FINDING
~~MR. RIGHT~~
MYSELF

NANDINI DHANANI

Become
Shakespeare
.com

First published in 2019 by

Becomeshakespeare.com

Wordit Content Design & Editing Services Pvt Ltd
Unit - 26, Building A-1, Nr Wadala RTO, Wadala (East),
Mumbai 400037, India
T:+91 8080226699

©

ISBN - 978-93-88930-05-5

I dedicate this book to my parents
Narain and Sushila Sawlani.

ACKNOWLEDGEMENTS

I would like to thank my Master Baba Hiral Shah for his grace and blessings. I am also grateful to my parents; Narain and Sushila, my husband; Lal and my children Sanam, Vinet, Chand and Armaan for their unconditional love and support. I would like to extend a special 'Thank you,' to my daughter, Sanam for editing my work.

Sandeep Adnani, my critic and guide. My friend, Shloka Bhatia, for encouraging me throughout my writing and procrastinating days.

I would also like to extend my gratitude to my editor; Nidhi Kaushik.

ABOUT THE AUTHOR

Nandini Dhanani was born in Mumbai, raised in Dubai and lived in Malaga, Spain.

She currently lives in Mumbai.

Wife of a businessman and mother to three kids, Nandini has always put the family at the apex of her priorities. They have been her learning curve.

Nandini's writings have appeared in a local English newspaper 'Sur' in Malaga and has served as a celebrity columnist for an Indian magazine 'Aaina' popular in the Balearic region.

In Mumbai, she made a significant contribution as an educator at Podar International School.

Her cross culture influences have helped shape Nandini's writing sensibilities. After experimenting in script writing, her passion stirred her to write fictional literature which brings us to her debut book.

PROLOGUE

Heart palpitating, nerves ticking, I woke up to the deafening scream that pierced through the darkness of the night. Fear gripped me by its horns; a muscular one-eyed man chased me with a packet of cocaine in one hand and a gun in the other. I tossed and turned in the pitch-dark room trying to get a wink, as the double bed squeaked every time I turned.

Switching on the night lamp, I hauled myself out of the bed towards the tiny kitchen, adjacent to the room. The tube-light flickered as I switched it on and I helped myself to the tap water. Staring at the clock that read 3 am, I gulped the cold water and slowly walked towards the living room. Four years of my life in London sat crammed in two suitcases on the wooden flooring. The only frame that I was leaving behind was of this fair-skinned muscular man who was smiling back at me. The smile that had exuded pleasure a week ago was irking me now. A sudden surge of rage had me pick up the metal frame and smash it against the wall. Covered with shattered glass, my boyfriend lay on the floor of the living room where we had spent many a nights dining, laughing, smoking, drinking and making love.

'Enough of your independence, it's time to settle down. Your lifestyle is unacceptable to us,' my mother screamed over *the phone. A live-in boyfriend whose existence I had hidden from the family had them enraged. I knew, I shouldn't have shared my secret with my only sibling Sonali; mother of two kids and untrustworthy.*

In moments of fear, the only people that cross your mind are your family and learning the truth about Alfredo made me fearful.

My parents wanted me back home, under their supervision and guidance. Attraction to an Italian man was unacceptable. The fault lay in my craving for physical satisfaction. My senses were drawn towards the man with whom a future would have been impossible. A strong headed and defiant man, whose body smelt of musk and a combination of weed and alcohol. His narrow blood shot eyes and raspy voice penetrated deep into my senses.

I was lonely, and Alfredo was not only charming, but also a kind-hearted soul who cooked and cleaned my home while I worked through the day. Unfortunately, the holiday had come to an end, so had my independence.

1

*"We don't meet people by accident. They are meant
to cross our path for a reason. Every person is a new door
to a different world." - Anonymous*

Mumbai

The 737 landed with a loud thud at the tarmac
of Chatrapati Shivaji International Airport,
screeching and gliding on the runway. The inability
to contain my pain had me spill the beans to my
only sister. Expecting secrecy from Sonali was far-
fetched; experiences from childhood had proven
this umpteen times. Yet, I repeated my mistakes. My
precariousness had caused me misery but giving it
up was not easy for me. Families are people with
whom one can share their pain and sorrow, but my
family was different.

'Priya you are so dark, consider yourself lucky that
a fair guy like Gaurav has agreed to marry you. It
is Babaji's blessings that you also are going into an
affluent family like your sister's.'

Babaji was my mother's Master and according to my
mother, his blessings were the only reason that we
were wealthy and happy. At the age of twenty-three,
I was engaged to Gaurav; who was twenty-seven

and lived off his father's wealth. Gaurav was a self-obsessed party animal who had me on my toes, during the two months of our engagement period. The only person who supported me was my grand-father who tried to reason with my parents. But my mother; wore the pants in our house and my father remained silent.

The night before our wedding functions commenced, I caught Gaurav smooching my best friend Pamela.

'You cannot break off your engagement for such a small matter. Gaurav must have been drunk; it is normal for men to waiver a bit. Think of the luxurious life you will be living,' my mother reasoned.

I fled to London that night with my grandfather's support and a lesson learnt. Never trust your friends. Pamela and I had been close friends since childhood, while Cristina had been my roommate in University. Cristina went out of her way to help me overcome the grief I was going through, letting me stay in her apartment till I found myself a job.

'Miss Priya Wadhwani, you just dropped your passport,' a melodious voice made me stop short from rushing towards the long immigration queue with my hand covering my nose to avoid the unbearable, stale musty stench of carpet.

I turned around, moving my hand away from my nose. A tall fair- skinned man held my passport, looking at me with his deep hazel eyes twinkling, as he handed it back to me.

'I am Ajai Mirchandani,' said the young man. The 'ani' surname meant he was a Sindhi. My mother would have jigged in joy.

'Thank you so much,' I responded with glee.

We were now walking in sync towards the immigration. As I checked my passport, my eyes spotted the Gucci loafers this man was wearing.

'I hope I haven't dropped anything else,' I muttered.

'I am pretty sure that was all that fell,' he replied.

'On holiday?' I asked.

'On a mission to be married,' said Ajai.

'Second marriage,' I jested.

Ajai unconsciously ran his fingers through the grey streaks as he stared blankly at me.

'I am sorry. I was just joking,' I responded in defence.

'Wiser and ready for marriage,' he winked.

'Witty answer.'

'I turned thirty-seven last week, to be precise.'

I am ten years younger than Ajai. My mind was already calculating.

The immigration officer stared at the picture on my passport and then at me.

'Old picture,' he said.

'Not too old. See the issue date. It's been only five years.'

The man instructed me to look at the camera. I had no idea whether I was supposed to grin or stand with a straight face. Unlike my friends who knew exactly how to pose for a flash; I stood there till the immigration officer handed me my passport after stamping it. I sauntered towards the luggage belt, as I dumped my passport in my handbag. From the corner of my eye, I watched Ajai stop by the duty free shop. Inserting my Indian number, I switched on my mobile. As soon as it started, a call from my mother flashed on the screen, "Monster mum".

'Where are you Priya? I am tired of waiting, how much longer?'

'Mum, I am at the luggage belt, they haven't yet loaded our baggage.'

'Okay, hurry up.'

She hung up.

How the hell am I supposed to hurry up? I mumbled under my breath. My mother had a knack of ticking a nerve that got me agitated. I stood there for approximately fifteen minutes and my phone had beeped thrice.

'Has your luggage arrived?' my mother messaged. I did not respond. The bell at the conveyor belt buzzed and the baggage was finally loaded. I glanced around, looking for Ajai but couldn't see him amongst the many passengers standing around.

My large blue bag with flower designs was finally visible. I waited for it to come closer, only to realize that it had been tampered with. My bra was hanging out of the suitcase along with a few panties peeking out. I lifted up the bag, only to find the handle in my hand, the bag moved further away. I ran towards it but missed it at the curve.

Out of nowhere, appeared Ajai and he hauled the thirty kilo suitcase from the belt and onto my trolley. *Two favours in a day*, I thought to myself.

'These Chinese bags,' I grumbled as Ajai glided his black Samsonite onto his trolley.

"Premiere class" read the tag on Ajai's luggage.

'My mum is freaking out. I need to rush,' I said, as I sprinted away.

Ajai followed me with his trolley as we walked through customs, placing our bags on the conveyor belt for scanning. Ajai was questioned for carrying four bottles of whiskey. Budging in, I informed the officer that two were from my allowance and moved them to my trolley.

'We're even,' I commented as I bid Ajai adieu.

Dressed in a red floral top, holding on to a Michael Kors handbag with Dior sunglasses perched on her long nose and chiselled face, I spotted mum.

'Two minutes longer and I would have had a heat stroke,' greeted mum. Scanning me as we walked towards the car in the scorching heat, she continued, 'You look so burnt out Priya.'

'It's sunny,' I responded to her illogical statement.

With no further comments, we headed silently to the car.

From the corner of my eye, I watched Ajai get into a car with a slightly aged woman.

'Whiskey for Dad, ha?' asked mother peering into the duty free bag.

'It's not mine. Oh God! It belonged to this guy I met at the immigration. I forgot to return it,' realisation dawned a wee bit late.

'Do you know him?'

'No, we just met.'

I wanted to spare the details of my interaction with him.

'Why would you co-operate with a total stranger?'

'Mum, he was a nice young man.'

'How old?' questioned my curious mother.

'I don't know mum,' I lied to avoid further probing.

Thankfully Rajan arrived with our Toyota Etios and I helped him store the luggage. My mother waited till Rajan came forward to open the door. I plugged in my headphones to avoid any further banter. The sweet voice of Arijit Singh helped me calm my nerves.

2

'*The heart of a mother is a deep abyss, at the bottom of which you will always find forgiveness.*'
- *Honore de Balzac*

'How are you Priya?' I woke up to my father's gruff voice.

Giving me a hug, dad sat on the chair beside the desk. My eyes adjusted to the morning light. Holding on to a few tissues, wiping his running nose, dad inquired about my well-being. I was praying that he would not begin asking me questions about Alfredo and my relationship with him.

'You can join my business, if you wish to,' dad said, as he sneezed for the tenth time.

Before my mind processed the information, my dad got busy with a business call and left the room yelling at his manager. Since childhood, the only time I ever heard my dad speak or scream was when he addressed his staff.

'Handling labourers is not an easy task,' was his general remark, '*I speak enough in the office. When I come home, I need to unwind. I don't want to listen to your frivolous banter.'* The statement would cause a friction and mum and dad would end up fighting with each other.

Dad was back after disconnecting his call, justifying himself. 'Sorry, I have a bunch of nincompoops to deal with at work. I am mentally exhausted, handling the staff is arduous and to top it the long hours of commute.'

I nodded in agreement as dad continued complaining.

'The traffic in Mumbai is insane and getting worse by the day. Priya, you have made a mistake by coming back to this country.'

'I thought, you all wanted me back here,' I interjected.

'Priya, you are an adult and we expected you to be more mature. If you end up in a wrong relationship, along with you we too suffer. Sonali told us about your Italian boyfriend and his drug abuse.'

I wanted to smack my sister.

'Your mother and I want to see you settled,' said dad.

I was in no mood to talk about Alfredo and my mistake, so instead I geared the conversation towards dad's work.

'You should retire now dad. Maybe you could spend more time with mum. Go for holidays. You have worked long enough.'

'With your mum?' Dad sniggered, 'It's difficult

to spend an hour with your mother, if I had to spend twenty-four hours, I would be heading to an asylum.'

'Are you complaining about me?' My mother barged into the room wearing a dark brown mud mask.

'No Radhika, I was not,' said dad, 'I was just telling Priya that how difficult it was to deal with people in India. Our roads are filled with potholes; the air here is unbreathable.'

'What are you complaining about Kamal? You travel to work in a chauffeur driven Mercedes.'

'If you did it for two consecutive days Radhika, you would be sitting at home with a broken back.'

'Come on Kamal, stop complaining all the time. Be positive, be grateful that you are not commuting in trains.'

'It's easy for you to be positive, Radhika. Your life is a blessing, no doubt. Morning kitty, lunch kitty, coffee kitty, birthday brunches and now your girls' night outs. If I had this kind of life, I doubt, I'd complain.'

'You are the man of the house and it's your duty to bring bread to the table.'

'And what about your duties?'

'You get your food on time, your bed is done. What's the matter?'

'Your staff does that.'

'So? Don't you have staff at work?'

'You need to support your man.'

'I am running the house for you, and if you think running a home is easy then please do it yourself.'

'Please, can you two not start again,' I budged in.

In their, thirty seven years of marriage instead of growing old together, mom and dad had drifted apart.

My mother had outgrown pleasing dad whenever he was upset; her attitude from love had transformed itself into indifference. The only time they were on the same page was during Sonali's wedding when they beamed with pride and joy to see their first daughter getting married into an affluent family.

'Wake up and call your sister,' screamed my mother after dad left the room in a huff.

Instead of following her instructions to call my sister, I sent a friend request to Ajai Mirchandani on facebook. Ajai was quick to accept the request. An invitation for lunch followed and I rushed into the washroom.

'What toothpaste is this, Mum? It tastes like shit.' I barged into my parent's extensive room. Laying on the chaise lounge with her face pack washed away, my mother was typing on her iPad.

'A toothpaste with no chemicals. Healthy for your

gums,' she answered as she looked up from the gadget.

'Bullshit,' I slurred, looking at my pyjama stained with red froth.

'Please go back to the bathroom before you mess the floor,' she yelled.

'Healthy! Whoever heard of toothpaste being healthy!'

My mother called out to Supriya to clean the mess that I left behind on her Italian Botticino. We had been mum's guinea pigs since childhood. Supriya was quick to catch on to mother's health plans and handed me a glass of vegetable juice.

'What the hell is this...some witch concoction?' I spat.

Tittering on her way out, Supriya banged into my mother.

'This is a green mixture to flush out toxins from your body,' barked mother.

Another advice from one of her socialite friends, I gathered.

'Mum, everything you suggest is not always right.'

'Correct that tone of yours, whatever I do is for your good.'

'How is a green concoction and a tasteless toothpaste good for me? If I may ask?'

'Sonali has it every day, that's why her skin looks young.'

'Sonali was born with a fair flawless skin. I was born wheatish and am prone to freckles. Sonali has your genes and I have dad's.'

Since childhood, I had been baked with talcum powder to make my skin fairer. Gram flour along with milk was rubbed everyday on my skin, but nothing changed my colour. Instead, it only made me detest my mother.

I emerged out of my room after an hour. My mother was in the kitchen bickering with our cook Ramu for using too much oil in the food.

'Where are you going Priya?' asked mother impatiently. Without turning around, I stepped out of the threshold, 'I have to return the bottles to the man from the airport.'

'You can send it across with the driver.' Now my mother was at the main door, while I stepped into the lift to avoid any further confrontation.

'Ajai has invited me for lunch at Taj Lands.'

'And what about the lunch I have cooked for you?'

'I can eat it for dinner.'

'I canceled my plans to spend time with you.'

'You didn't have to mum.'

'You are so insensitive Priya,' complained mum.

I shut the lift door.

3

"You cannot always wait for the perfect time.
Sometimes you must dare to jump." - Anonymous

Ajai stood by the red and gold embellished pillar at the entrance of the eatery in the hotel. Disconnecting his phone, Ajai greeted me with two kisses on my cheek.

'Your parcel.' I handed Ajai his two bottles of whiskey.

He held my hand and said, 'How about starting with a hello.'

'Hello Ajai Mirchandani,' I responded with a smile.

'Hello Ms. Priya Wadhwani.'

The usher guided us to our table.

'I am so sorry, I didn't intend to bother you with this,' said Ajai as he held on to the duty-free bag. 'It was very kind of you to trace me on Facebook and message. In all honesty, I had forgotten your surname.'

'Wadhwani.'

'Of course, I know it now. I saw it when you messaged.'

The waiter handed us the drinks menu as we sat beside the French windows.

'I sincerely apologize. I should have offered to send my chauffeur to collect the bottles.'

'Maybe you should have.'

'But I wouldn't get a chance to know a beautiful woman like you,' Ajai complimented as he pulled the black chair for me to be seated.

'You're a charmer and a flirt.'

Ajai's smile widened as he spoke, 'Charmer yes, flirt not too sure.'

The flirtations were interrupted with the arrival of Ajai's mother.

Dressed in beige linen trousers and a white shirt, she greeted me with a cold handshake. 'Nice to meet you aunty,' I greeted.

'You can call me Kamini,' she said in a gentle voice, which was in contrast to her stern look.

Holding on to my hand, Kamini scanned me from top to bottom. The scanner that every woman has ingrained in her brain, judging my unpedicured feet, my chipped nails and the paunch that stuck out of my trousers.

'What do you do Priya?' asked Kamini.

'Mum please sit down,' said Ajai pulling up a chair for his mother.

'Aunty, I worked as a financial advisor in London.'

'You were in London. How is it we never saw you at any event?'

How I wished I could tell her that I detested Indians abroad. Being evasive, I just puckered my lips.

'It looks like it's going to rain,' Kamini commented looking outside the window where dark clouds had gathered.

Her eyes were once again fixated on me. The icy stare in Kamini's hazel eyes was intimidating. Mirroring Kamini, I sipped on the glass of water.

How many of you are there in your house? What does your father do? What does your mother do? Kamini's grilling session had me look out for Ajai who had disappeared on his mother's arrival.

Not too pleased to hear that my mother was a Punjabi. From family questions she moved on to my beliefs.

'Whom do you worship?'

'Worship? No one,' I responded.

'You are an atheist?'

'No. It's not that I don't believe in God. I believe in

the power of the Universe. I just don't believe in idol worship, I believe in goodness.'

Kamini raised her brows and before she could argue, Ajai was back and informed his mother that he had arranged the hotel car for her to meet her family in Thane.

My face lit up to know that the woman was leaving.

'Sorry beta, I have to leave,' said Kamini.

I wanted to whirl in joy like the Sufi dervishes. The women had *pakaoed* me with her non-stop questions. While Ajai escorted his mother to the car, I watched the dark clouds hover on the rough grey sea as I hummed to myself, *'barso re megha barso re megha barso.'*

'Someone is enjoying their own company,' said Ajai.

'I hope it rains.'

'It looks like it will,' said Ajai as he called for the waiter.

'Hot and sour soup, chicken in black bean sauce and garlic fried rice, spiced with red chillies,' I ordered, while Ajay grinned and added stir fried vegetables for himself.

'I am sorry but I am starving, I have not eaten since last night.'

'Why is that?'

'Because my mother fed me a witch concoction instead of breakfast.'

Ajai's eyes widened as he asked, 'Are you serious?'

'Yes, mother and me share a love-hate relationship.'

I narrated the episode in my life where my mother had sprayed my hair with Hit - insect killer to exterminate the lice that had invaded my crowning glory.

'I guess that's the secret to your beautiful dark hair,' said Ajai.

'I think otherwise. It's a miracle that I have any hair left on my head.'

'Did she spray your hair often with the pesticide?'

'Thankfully no. My father educated mother of her foolishness.'

'You mean innocence.'

'Possibly innocent as she is easily influenced by her socialite friends. She tends to suck up to them and follows their advise blindly.'

'She must have lots of friends?' asked Ajai.

'She is a social butterfly, hopping from one party to another,' I responded.

'If that makes her happy, why not,' said Ajai.

'Happiness is a state of mind as they say. She finds her happiness with friends, so be it.'

'I never saw it that way. I find social life a waste of time. These parties and friends are all a farce,' I responded, as the waiter served our lunch.

I watched Ajai nibble on carrots and cucumber, while I drank my soup.

'Are you dieting?' I asked.

'Not dieting but yes, I am careful with my diet,' said Ajai.

'I thought only women were obsessed with diets.'

'How can I meet my prospect with a bulging stomach? She would reject me instantly.'

'It's strange how we focus more on the physical features instead of connecting mentally and soulfully,' I added.

'I agree Priya. But I cannot find myself connecting to anyone soulfully anymore.' 'I had found my soul mate,' said Ajai, as he stared at my empty soup bowl.

'How lovely,' I responded, 'and where is she now?'

'She is no more,' responded Ajai, his eyes now gazing at some far away object in the restaurant.

'I am so sorry. What happened?'

'She died in a car accident.'

'How?'

Two weeks prior to our wedding, Suzie had driven

to Birmingham to visit her ailing father and seek his blessings. The car tyre burst and the car slid and crashed onto the railings on the highway,' Ajai mumbled.

It felt odd to console a stranger, but I held Ajai's hand trying to comfort him of his pain. The pain that had not healed despite the incident happening a few years ago. True love never dies.

The love that he exuded for Suzie brought about a tinge of envy in my stomach. It felt good to know that there were men out there who loved selflessly, unlike the men I had met in my life.

'The pain is still alive somewhere deep within me, the only difference is that with time I have learned to cope with it,' said Ajai placing his right hand on his heart. 'In some ways she was like you Priya. Innocent and funny,' Ajai added under his breath.

Did he just say I was innocent and funny like Suzie? Funny like Suzie possible, but innocent? That was one term no one in my family used for me. They called me moody, irritable, and selfish. Funny was a term that my friends used occasionally but innocent never. Although, it felt good. If only Ajai knew of the sudden desire that had crept up within me. He would never have called me innocent.

'What about the girls you will be meeting?'

Ajai tapped on his iPhone, 'This is Sonakshi,' he said as he handed his phone to me.

Sonakshi was posing beside a tree, with highlighted hair, tons of make- up and fair skin.

'Wow. She is gorgeous.'

'I have been in touch with Sonakshi for two weeks. We have been chatting on and off, she is sweet. My mother is very fond of her as she is a pro in cooking and is educated and well mannered.'

Did he just say mother? Why were men obsessed with their mothers?

'That's Sejal,' said Ajai as he swiped his gallery pictures.

A petite wheatish skinned girl, with jet black hair styled in a blunt cut, stood against a wall.

'She is cute,' I grinned.

'She is very intelligent and well-read. I like her maturity, but my mother prefers Sonakshi.'

'Why mother? Shouldn't it be about your preference, instead of your mother's,' I asked.

'I would do anything for my mother's happiness. My mother has sacrificed a lot for us. We lost our father when we were young, if it was not for my mother, I would have committed suicide after Suzie's death.

No comments would be a better choice at this moment.

Ajai ate his stir fried vegetables slowly while I devoured the spicy chicken and rice.

The rains were now lashing hard, on the French windows.

'How about experiencing the first rains in Mumbai?' I asked.

'I am not too fond of the monsoon season. Nor do I wish to fall sick.'

'You have to experience the rain. C'mon don't be a spoil sport.'

After a lot of convincing, Ajai agreed and we walked out of the hotel to the promenade and I jumped onto the rocks.

'Are you crazy? It's dangerous to be out there. Come back up Priya,' Ajai shouted .

'Do you fear death?' I asked stretching out my right hand. Running his long fingers through his wet hair, Ajai stood silently.

'Don't be so boring Ajai?' I teased, suddenly losing my balance as I spoke. Ajai instantly grabbed my hand, preventing me from falling.

'You are crazy Priya,' said Ajai as he too jumped onto the rocks.

'We all are crazy Ajai,' I responded as I hopped onto another rock towards the stormy waves.

'It's too cold and dangerous to be on these rocks,' said Ajai following my lead.

Standing on a huge rock I lifted my face to the clouds

above. The touch of rain felt like a direct blessing from the Universe.

'I love the gentle touch of rain, don't you?' I whispered, as I turned towards Ajai.

Without responding to my question, Ajai wrapped his arms around me.

I held him by his waist as he lost balance. Our fingers entwined, as we stood still for a while on a flat rock staring at the stormy sea. The salty breeze and the rain worked its magic on us. Drawing closer towards Ajai, our lips met and I let my desire transform into action. His touch aroused a temptation that I was unwilling to let go of.

4

"Money does not change people, it unmasks them"
- Anonymous

Three days later...

Ajai's facebook status read 'Engaged', and pictures of the couple brandishing their rings were posted. Gleaming with joy in a mauve *salwar kameez*, Sonakshi displayed the huge rock on her finger. I swiped to the family picture where everyone was grinning. Kamini stood beside her to be fair skinned daughter-in-law, on one side and Ajai in a light blue *kurta pyjama*, on the other.

My mobile rang, flashing the name, Ritika.

The moment I answered, 'You idiot, you are in Mumbai and you haven't yet called me,' screamed Ritika; my childhood friend.

'I just arrived a few days back Ritika. I am still jet lagged.'

'I don't care. You could have atleast texted.' I was in no mood to chat with anyone, not even to my best friend. 'Ritika, can I call you back please,' and without waiting for her reply, I disconnected.

My mind was disturbed with the fact that Ajai was

engaged to Sonakshi. Something within had changed after we had kissed each other. I had hoped that Ajai would call off the engagement.

My mind relived the kiss, Ajai and I shared as I lit a cigarette.

Ajai had not messaged or called since he left for Jaipur and I wondered if he would ever call me again.

The slight drizzle unearthed the scent of wet soil, that was nostalgic of the times when as children we rushed under the torrent, penetrating our skins, moistening us as we danced in bliss. The pleasures derived from small things as a child were long forgotten once one crossed the threshold. Adulthood was all about responsibilities and heartbreaks. The rains that had been witness to the moment of ecstasy and joy I had felt in Ajai's arms. The lingering taste of the salty breeze after Ajai and I walked away bidding an awkward good bye. I inhaled and exhaled the nicotine, while watching myself being consumed with emotions of jealousy. Jealousy that was making my mind restless and polluted. My grandfather would have said that *its this emotion that kills all the nobility and humanity in the heart of the sufferer*. I detested Sonakshi despite not meeting her.

The pain within had my body crumble bit by bit, my temples hurt. Ajai had played havoc with my mind and he wasn't even aware. Or was he? I was not as angry at Ajai as I was with Sonakshi for usurping what could have been my right. I was the victim and Sonakshi the culprit.

'You are smoking *masi*?' said my seven year old nephew Aaryan.

Shocked to see my nephew standing on the terrace, I flicked the cigarette.

'You are harming the environment by smoking and littering,' he added.

Surprised with my young nephew's knowledge, said sheepishly, 'You are right Aaryan. I am sorry.'

'My teacher says that smoking kills.'

I wish it did, for I was behaving like a child whose new toy had been snatched away.

I hugged Aaryan tightly for a minute and let out a whimper.

'Are you crying *masi*?'

I couldn't respond.

'I am sorry *masi*, I didn't mean to hurt you,' said Aaryan as he wiped a tear.

'I am sorry Aaryan, for being so bad.'

'You are not bad *masi*. Your action was wrong,' said Aaryan holding me tightly in his little arms.

'I never seem to do anything right in my life.'

'Mum says, we all make mistakes, but we must learn from our mistakes.'

'Your mum is always right Aaryan. She always says

and does the right things,' I said, as I pecked Aaryan on his cheek.

Wiping his cheek he informed me that Sonali was waiting for me.

'Tell mum, I'll be there in few minutes.'

'There you are Madam,' said Sonali, greeting me with a hug as I walked into the living room. '

'Please don't smoke in front of my children,' whispered Sonali.

'He already lectured me on that,' I informed her about Aaryan's comments and she smiled.

'IB schools make a difference. They teach a child to think and question.'

'International schools are expensive. Aren't they?' I asked.

'Yes, they are. But International schools not only provide good education, they also help in networking. My children's classmates are from influential families and a relationship with them will help them in the future.'

'How?'

'To find good jobs,' said Sonali.

'I would have never thought of schools being the ground for networking.'

'The friendships you build in those years last forever,' said Sonali.

In a way Sonali was right, I shared a deep bond with my childhood friend Ritika. We always caught up from where we left. Sometimes we didn't speak for months yet there was a connection. Instead of calling my sister, if I had called Ritika I would not have been back home.

I turned my attention to Aashna who was busy playing games on the iPad. Aashna ignored me as I greeted her.

'Leave the gadget and say hello to *masi*,' instructed Sonali.

Keeping the iPad aside Aashna gave me a peck on my cheek and sprinted back.

'Where's mum?' I asked Sonali.

'She is in the kitchen organizing snacks for her grand-children.'

'She loves her grand-children more than she loved us.'

'Yes, she never entered the kitchen for us,' winked Sonali.

Sonali was a busy mother running from one class to another with her children, besides attending kitty parties.

'The children had a holiday today, so I thought I might as well drop in. And then I find out you are still sleeping.'

'I was just lazing,' I added.

'Any news from the druggie?' asked Sonali.

'I have blocked him,' I curtly replied.

'I know you must be upset that I involved mum and dad. But they needed to know the truth. I was scared that Alfredo might harm you and you wouldn't listen to me.'

'This is not the first time you have snitched on me Sonali,' I smirked.

Sonali had snitched on me on many occasions. The memory that stayed forever was when I informed her of visiting Jimmy's home as his parents were travelling. I could not refuse Jimmy when he asked me to watch a movie with him in his house. An X-rated movie that he had managed to get on DVD. I was beaten black and blue by my mother.

'I only kissed him,' I had cried.

'You cannot kiss any boy. If you do wrong Babaji will punish you. You will be fried alive in hot oil,' warned mother.

From that day onwards, instead of loving Babaji, I feared him.

After the episode I had promised never to tell my sister anything.

'It was for your own good,' Sonali had said, while I seethed in pain. The pain that stayed imprinted in my heart. Once again, my sister proclaimed 'it was for your good.'

'Why do you end up in messy relationships?' Sonali queried as she filed her nail.

It was difficult to explain to my sister that it was not love that I was looking for with Alfredo. Our relationship was more need based, as living alone in London was difficult. I met Alfredo at a party where we smoked weed, danced, drank and ended up in my bedroom. The next obvious step was him moving into my apartment. We were friends with benefits. The fact that he was drug peddling was only known to me when the cops came in search of him. In a state of panic, I called Cristina who was then travelling, hence unavailable. So instead, I called my sister for advise.

My mum stepped out of the kitchen untying the strings of her apron, 'you see how she has put on so much weight. You are her sister tell her something. She does not listen to me.'

'Mum I do listen to you. I drank your witch's brew, didn't I?'

Sonali pleaded that I listen to mum and not argue.

'I listened to her, that is why I am here,' I sighed.

'You are here because you made a wrong choice,' yelled mum.

'I came here because you are my family. And the only thing I ask for is love. But instead of nurturing me, you berate me.'

'You have berated yourself Priya by having an affair

with an Italian guy. God knows what you have done with that druggie. Hope Babaji forgives you,' said mother as she folded her hands and bowed to her Master's large gold framed photograph in the living room.

'If you can't forgive me, how will your Babaji. And anyways I don't need your Babaji to forgive me or bless me. Last time it was thanks to your Babaji that I was engaged to Gaurav.'

The picture that once had stirred fear within, did not matter anymore. It was not Babaji but disciples like mother who instilled fear in their children in the hope that they would follow their religion and their beliefs.

Mum retorted, 'That was your *karma*, Priya.'

'When good happens it's Babaji, when bad happens it's my *karma*,' I screamed.

Mother headed to her room in a huff.

'You need to calm down Priya. This is not the way to talk to mum,' chided Sonali.

'And is it the right way for all of you to treat me? All the time you talk about my past, my skin, my weight. Have you all ever asked me about my work, my dreams, my ambitions?'

'You are not easy to talk to Priya.'

'That is so convenient Sonali.' 'We all love you Priya,' said Sonali as she embraced me.

'We care for you and whatever I say or do is for your

good. I am your older sister and whatever I do is to protect you. Please don't misunderstand me.'

Hearing her words, I calmed down instantly.

Supriya handed me the witch's concoction and I returned it.

'I want a chicken sandwich,' I barked, 'not this concoction.'

Supriya immediately retreated to the kitchen to give instructions to Ramu.

Just then, mum surfaced from her room wearing a long red dress, hair pinned up and her chandelier diamonds dazzling.

'Nice dress mum,' said Sonali with a smile.

'It's Bebe, I got it when I had gone with my friends to Hong Kong and check out my latest Hermes,' mum flaunted her bag and added, 'this also I bought on that trip. Everyone was buying, so I too decided to own one.'

'Dad must have freaked out,' said Sonali.

'He always does. He is a miser.'

While mother and Sonali discussed how dad was a miser and an anti-social human being, I checked my mobile for messages and revisited Ajai's facebook. No new pictures had been uploaded.

As soon as I had my chicken sandwich Sonali insisted that I go for a new look, a new me. 'You need to highlight your hair Priya and Botox it.'

'Botox?'

'Yes, it makes your hair silky,' she added.

'Yes maasi, your hair is very wavy,' Aashna dropped her iPad and touched my hair.

'I also want to wash my hair in the parlour,' said the seven year old.

'Like mum, like daughter,' I stated.

The visit to the salon lasted for four hours during which I checked my mobile umpteen times, hoping to receive a message from Ajai. As soon as I was home, mother clicked my picture and in twenty minutes had posted it on her facebook.

'Priya you look ravishing.' Read the comment below.

While mum commented, 'A new look, a new you.'

I barged into mum's room who was sitting on her chaise lounge chatting to Sonali while she photoshopped the pictures of her afternoon lunch kitty on her iPad.

'We live in the same house mum,' I yelled. 'You don't need to compliment me on facebook.'

'Sonali wants to talk to you,' said mother as she handed me her mobile phone, ignoring my remark.

My sister's enthusiasm for life splashed its way through the phone. Her tone was always musical and engaging, 'I hear you are getting a lot of compliments.'

I crinkled my nose.

'Thank you for the transformation and the three likes from you, mum and my dear brother-in-law, Vinodji.'

From taking credit for my new look, to talking about her social connections, my sister's blabbering had me curse the moment I had walked into my mother's room.

Sonali had set up a dinner plan with her friend, Deepa Bhatia and her family. Deepa's son was an eligible bachelor and Sonali believed that he was my Mr.Right.

'They are extremely wealthy,' added Sonali.

I tittered at Sonali's comment.

'Why are you laughing?' asked Sonali.

'You are asking me to see a guy because he is wealthy.'

'What's wrong in that? You're not going to marry some middle class working guy. Are you?'

'What's wrong with marrying a middle class guy? Love is what counts, not wealth.'

'Love flies out of the window when there is no money.'

'Are you implying that attraction and companionship does not matter?'

'Priya, sex is secondary. Comfort should be your priority.'

'Who said anything about sex?'

'I am not meeting anyone,' I announced.

'You cannot waste your life like this. Mum and dad are worried about your future Priya.'

'They don't need to worry, I can fend for myself.'

'You are our responsibility and we need to complete it before we die,' said mother.

Handing the phone to mother, I stomped out of the room and sulked in my locked room.

After an hour of sulking I was forced out of my room. 'Open the door Priya, its dinner time,' called dad as he knocked on the door.

The dinner was silent, till mother brought out the topic of Deepa Bhatia.

'Why do we have to tag along? Let them meet on their own,' dad argued with mother.

'That is how they want it. We're the girl's side and we can't afford to not comply as your daughter isn't getting younger.'

'Has Sonali met the boy before? How does he look? What does he do?' asked my inquisitive father. Thankfully, he was asking questions.

'We will find out tomorrow, Kamal.'

'Radhika, this is about our daughter. We need to know about the boy before meeting him.'

'Kamal could you just leave it to us?'

'But Radhika....'

'Just go with the flow,' mum didn't let dad complete his sentence.

Sonali and mum controlled the reigns of their homes. Refusing to be a part of mother-daughter symphony, dad headed to his room to watch the news.

'Tomorrow morning, you will go with Sonali to the mall,' barked mum.

Mum had ransacked my cupboard and unable to find anything decent to wear had instructed Sonali to take me shopping.

'For what?' I asked.

'To meet the Bhatia family.'

'When did I say that I was interested?' I snapped.

******

At eleven in the morning, dressed in a short beige dress, Bulgari shades covering her large eyes, Sonali rebuked me for not applying any lipstick, 'A woman should never step out without a dash of colour on her lips,' she remarked as we walked into a designer store at the mall.

I picked a dress that was disapproved by Sonali, 'you'll look big in this.'

'I am not big, I am healthy,' I responded, 'and if the boy rejects me on those grounds then it will be a blessing in disguise. I would not like to be married to someone who will judge me on my appearance.'

'First impressions do matter Priya.'

'Not for me,' I responded.

'I am sure if I asked you to chose between a healthy and a lean handsome guy, you would go for the handsome guy.'

'If only he had brains. I don't wish to marry some rich brainless guy.'

While I picked a dress for the evening, Sonali bought a few herself.

'When is Vinodji back from China?' I asked as Sonali strolled into Sephora.

'In a week.'

'Don't you miss him?'

Sonali tried the new lipstick shade on her skin.

'A little space in marriage is important. It gives me my me time, when he is travelling.'

'But you live with your in-laws.'

'They too are visiting their daughter in Bangalore.'

Sonali picked up a foundation and concealer for my skin saying, 'you need to hide those freckles,' while picking up a few shades of lipsticks for herself.

'They say we use one eighth of the makeup we buy,' I commented.

'I love owning the latest collection.'

'We own more than we need. Don't we?'

Ignoring my comment, Sonali paid the bill and we headed home.

******

Sonali had erased the flaws, contoured my nostrils and highlighted my face while Aashna watched her mother in awe. Her eyes twinkling with amazement, to see her aunt being transformed.

Irritated yet complying with my family wishes as they transformed me, we headed towards the venue.

Mother and Sonali constantly bickered and gossiped about their kitty friends while dad sat silently.

'Deepa is reaching in a few minutes,' Sonali announced, as we settled ourselves at the restaurant.

'Priya please be cordial and smile when they come in,' instructed my sister and my mother too added her bit, 'don't laugh loudly and don't order any hard drinks.'

Pretence was not something I was comfortable with and expecting a goody act from me was a mistake.

Three pairs of eyes were now gazing at the door.

'There they are!' Sonali muttered in delight as she pulled the drinks menu away from me.

I watched the family of three, parade towards the table, all walking in a symmetrical line. A bulky woman carrying a Hermes bag, wearing an animal print blue and brown kaftan top with brown leggings.

She was followed by a gaunt boy and a pot- bellied bald man.

Avinash Bhatia, aged thirty was dressed in Armani jeans and a black Moschino shirt barely covering the gold chains hung around his neck.

'Hi, I'm Avinash Bhatia,' he said, extending his sweaty hand with a diamond bracelet encircling his wrist, and his fingers, laden with rings studded with different coloured stones.

'I thought, you were Avinash Zaveri.'

My mother coughed loudly.

'No, it's Bhatia.'

I obviously knew he was a Bhatia but watching his mother and him sparkle in diamonds reminded me of the diamond market in Mumbai.

'So Priya, what do you do?' asked Deepa as she seated herself opposite me and signalled Avinash to sit on my left.

'Nothing,' I bluntly replied.

'Nothing? I thought you are working in a big firm in London.'

'I was working in London. Not in a big firm though. Now I am on a sabbatical, spending lost time with family.'

My family always distorted facts and I could imagine how they would have spoken highly of me to Deepa.

'You are a homely girl then.'

'I wouldn't call myself homely.'

My mother and sister looked at me in dismay.

'You aren't?' Deepa's eyes seemed larger than her body.

'With all due respect Mrs. Bhatia, homely means ugly. I don't consider myself ugly.' Hoping that my sense of humour would garner a few laughs and a compliment.

Deepa sniggered only to hit me hard with her following remark.

'I wouldn't call you ugly, you're an average looking girl.'

'Aren't we all average?' I retorted. 'Your son too, is average looking.'

A kick on my shin had me shriek.

'Priya loves to joke,' said mum opening her eyes wide.

'You know Priya,' said Deepa, 'Avinash is one of the few eligible bachelors in Mumbai. There is a line of girls waiting to marry him.'

Deluded woman. I wanted to scream out loud.

What was with these wealthy families? Were they born with a distorted brain? Did they not perceive the world, as the world perceived them?

'Avinash is a gem. All the women in our kitty are eyeing him for their daughter,' Sonali butted.

'Seriou.......' The word stayed in the air, as another kick on my shin had me gasp for breath.

While I tried hard to contain my pain, Avinash blushed, as Sonali and mum showered him with praises.

'Aren't they lucky that they get to choose their partner. We had to be happy with what our parents chose for us,' Deepa snortled as she glanced at her husband.

Munching on the starters Mr. Bhatia and father discussed the country's economy. Mrs. Bhatia, Sonali and mum discussed kitty issues with a passion.

Avinash intervened, to remind his mother of the time when her kitty friend had robbed her mobile.

'I once played cards with these women. I always warned her about this particular woman. And lo, she turned out to be what I predicted. A thief,' said Avinash.

'What do you do for a living, Avinash?' I asked Avinash.

'Avinash is born with a golden spoon. He does not need to work as our income comes from the wise investments my husband has made in the past. He does go to office once in a while and invests in the share market as well Mrs.Bhatia responded.'

Were all boys under their mother's influence or was it I, who was destined to meet those kind.

'We have so much by Babaji's grace that Avinash does not need to work,' Deepa announced as she dipped her piece of onion pancake into the chilli sauce.

'Babaji is quite biased towards you,' I jested.

A kick from my mother was enough to rile me.

'My mother too is a follower of Babaji and insists I eat vegetarian food or Babaji will punish me. But I don't believe in all this. I have nothing to do with Babaji. I like non-veg food and enjoy my drinks. It's only out of respect that I am eating a veg meal, today,' I responded, moving my legs behind the chair where mum's legs would not reach mine.

'But she will give up after marriage,' my mother interrupted.

Deepa's nose flared as her breasts moved upwards and downwards in agony.

'Did you just insult my Babaji?'

'I did not insult,' I responded.

Sonali intervened, 'We all are followers of Babaji. Priya loves to joke.'

Deepa stood up and suddenly a loud argument diverted our attention.

Mr. Bhatia was rebuking at the waiter for picking up his plate, 'How dare you touch my plate, while I am still eating?'

'But Sir, the plate is empty. I was getting you a fresh one for the main course.'

'Look at my mouth, it's still moving,' the stout man yelled pointing towards his moving mouth.

The waiter was apologetic, yet he continued snubbing him.

'Mr. Bhatia you are over reacting; he was only doing his job,' I said.

Twelve pair of eyes reprimanded me at my statement, instantly.

The dinner ended with the Bhatia family rejecting me and calling me the black sheep of the family. My parents and sister watched in silence.

My family ignored me on the ride back home.

Feeling lonely and isolated, I dialled Ritika's number but her phone was switched off. A message from Ajai lifted my spirits.

'I am engaged,' read the message, 'Congratulations!' I responded.

'Are you free to chat?' he asked.

5

*"According to the Hindu way of thinking, marriage is
rather a duty than a privilege."*
- Swami Vivekananda

'How dare you take my plate away?'

'Sir your plate was empty.'

'But my mouth is full, can't you see it moving. How
can you take my plate when my mouth is still moving?'

Ajai cackled watching me imitate Mr. Bhatia. Last
evening, Ajai had been kind enough to respond. He
was at the Jaipur airport when I called him. Listening
patiently, as I poured my heart out while he waited
for his flight from Jaipur to Mumbai. When he finally
landed in Mumbai, he called me to meet him.

'Your expressions are priceless. You should have been
in the movies,' said Ajai as we sat in the coffee shop..

'As a vamp?'

'No not at all. As a comedian.'

'Are you serious? My family believes, I am the most
khadoos person on earth.'

'Maybe you wear a façade when you are with your family. There must be some episode that has created bitterness within you and it surfaces in their presence. But I am sure that at heart, you are a compassionate soul,' said Ajai with a smile.

My eyes fixated at his lips as he spoke, my heart melted and my knees gave way. I wanted the moment to freeze so that Ajai could sing my praises. For once, someone was making me feel beautiful inside out.

'I actually missed you in Jaipur,' said Ajai.

The random statement caught me off guard.

If only I could ask him, if he missed me the way I missed him.

'The way your nose crinkles when you speak, your eyes narrow and widen, your forehead creases,' Ajai jested.

'Hmm,' I responded, making sure I had no expression on my face.

After Ajai had finished his commentary, I stared at the huge solitaire diamond ring he was wearing. 'I am sorry I forgot to congratulate you, just realized you are engaged.'

Ajai flaunted his commitment. 'You saw the pictures on facebook?' he asked.

'I have not visited facebook,' I lied.

Ajai raised his brow.

'So, how is it to be engaged? Are you excited?' I asked.

Furrowing his lips, Ajai commented, 'I don't know it's still sinking in but my mother is thrilled.'

I had not asked him about his mother. I wanted to know about his feelings.

'She has already decided for a wedding in December and has stayed back in Jaipur to plan the destination and spend time with her, to be daughter-in-law.'

How was that possible? Sonakshi and Ajai had just met and spent three days with families circling around them. Like my engagement to Gaurav was doomed from day one. We never loved each other. It was an arrangement by our parents.

'Are you happy to be married so soon?' I asked, watching Ajai's expression to gauge his feelings.

Just when Ajai was about to respond, his mobile vibrated displaying Sonakshi's name. Ajai turned the mobile upside down.

'Aren't you going to answer?' I asked.

'I can speak to her later. It would be unfair to ignore the person sitting in front of me.'

My stomach jigged in joy to hear that Ajai had prioritized me over his fiancée.

Curious to know more about his fiancée I asked Ajai to describe Sonakshi.

'Sonakshi is beautiful and talented. She is highly educated and enjoys painting and singing. She sang a beautiful bhajan when we visited her home for dinner.'

How typical of these girls to flaunt their skills.

Pretending not to have seen his engagement pictures, I requested Ajai to share the pictures of his engagement. Ajai tapped on his gallery that had more than fifty pictures of the ceremony of which Ajai had only uploaded a few.

'I like your kurta pyjama. The colour suits you,' I added as I moved beside him to check the pictures. The musk fragrance filled my nostrils as his long slender fingers tapped on the pictures.

'Thank you. Honestly, I still cannot believe that I am engaged. Everything happened so quickly,' Ajai exclaimed as he stopped at the picture where Ajai was slipping a ring into Sonakshi's manicured fingers. 'In an hour of our meeting, the family had exchanged sweets.'

'How could you say yes in an hour?'

'My mother saw no reason to delay and her emotional outburst led to us exchanging rings the next day in the temple.'

'Don't you have any wishes for yourself Ajai?'

Ajai was interrupted by a call from his mother. He walked away to return after a few minutes with the request to join him on his shopping spree. A list of things that his mother wanted him to take back to London.

Ajai forwarded me the list and I read through it. One kilo Sev barfi from Tharu at Khar market, list of savouries from Neelam stores, dry fruits from Royal Dry fruits on SV road and twenty-four artificial gold and silver bangles, bindis and mang tikka for Tina from Santacruz market. With an additional note to check out fancy clothes for the small idols of baby Krishna, Jhulelal, Lord Vishnu and Laxmi mata.

We commenced our shopping spree in a Toyota Corolla rented from the hotel. The sky was clear and high level of humidity had us perspiring as we walked out of the car to the savoury store that was popular for its farsan. After purchasing two bags of farsan, we headed to Khar market and bought jazzy wear for the gods. Ajai spoke of the full moon prayers that were a ritual in their home, where he and his mother woke up early in the morning to complete the prayer.

'Your mother is very religious,' I commented.

'Yes she is. She spends a lot of time in naam japa.'

'And you?'

'I lost faith in God after Suzie's death.'

'Your *karmic* account with her had come to an end. You cannot blame God or the Universe for the same. Death is but a beginning to a new life.'

'You are very spiritual,' said Ajai as I gobbled on the sweets that the shopkeeper offered to try. 'I like the *sev barfi*,' I responded.

Ajai instructed the shop keeper to pack a kilo for his mother and a kilo for me.

'My mother will freak out, if she finds this at home,' I chuckled.

On completion of the errands in Khar, we headed towards Santacruz market. The market was buzzing with hawkers selling wares on the pavement. We entered the store that Kamini had guided Ajai to visit, browsing through the variety of bangles that the shopkeeper exhibited. I jangled the bangles as Ajai asked me to try them on. Unable to slip them in, Ajai asked for a bigger size for me.

'They look good on you,' said Ajai as he helped me slip in the bigger size bangles.

I blushed with a, 'Thank you.'

'Do you like Indian wear?'

'No, not at all.'

'Have you worn a saree ever?'

'Not really,' I retorted.

'You should,' said Ajai. His eyes fixated on my bangles.

The words were spoken with so much conviction that I was ready to discard my jeans and change into a saree.

Moving on to the *mang tikka* section, Ajai chose a simple bronze oval shaped design.

'You look beautiful,' said Ajai as he placed it on my forehead.

He asked for two similar pieces to be kept aside.

Passing by the colourful mojris section that lay on the glass shelf, Ajai asked for a pair.

'Is it for your sister?' I asked.

'No, it's for you. It will look lovely on your feet.'

With great enthusiasm the salesman brought a pair and pulled it out of the box.

Ajai inspected the mojris and then bend on his knees to help me try them on. His touch on my skin had a current run up my spine. Slipping my feet into the mojris, I walked a few steps, ignoring the warm sensation that was building up within me.

'Are they comfortable?" asked Ajai.

'Yes,' I responded in a whisper, 'but I don't wear mojris.'

'You will for me,' he responded and ordered a pair for his sister too.

The car moved slowly through the congested market dodging, the swarm of people crossing and walking on the narrow road. Spotting a saree store, 'That was not on your mother's list.'

'It's on mine,' said Ajai as he sifted through the different textiles that ranged from Georgette to chiffons to satin.

Finally selecting a chiffon pistachio, digital printed pistachio saree.

The overenthusiastic salesman twirled around me as he draped the saree on me.

Ajai stood silently watching me, his eyes exuding a warmth that was igniting a spark within me.

Electrified with his own mastery at draping a saree, the pencil moustached salesman looked at Ajai for approval.

'It's too expensive. Ajai I cannot accept it.'

Ajai held my hand and walked me down the narrow staircase.

'Don't argue Priya,' said Ajai.

With the saree bag in Ajai's hand, we stepped outside the store to be greeted by thunder, lightning and rains. Huddled under an umbrella the watchman lent us, Ajai dialled the hotel chauffer. Unable to reach him, we hailed an auto rickshaw.

Ajai held on to me tightly as the driver dodged and speeded on the pot holed roads of Mumbai. Drawing closer, holding hands. After a few moments, Ajai touched his ring finger and moved away.

Stopping outside Starbucks, Ajai invited me for a coffee before we parted ways. Sipping on latte, as we watched the rains lambast the city.

'Have you ever been in love?' asked Ajai.

I had no answer to the question. *Did I ever love Jimmy or Gaurav or Alfredo?* Jimmy was a teenage crush like other crushes that I had had throughout my school year. Gaurav was my parent's choice, and Alfredo was a relationship of convenience and need. A realization dawned that I had actually never loved any of them.

'If I may ask, why did you break your engagement to Gaurav.'

'I caught him kissing my friend.'

'It could have been a moment of weakness. We humans do make mistakes.'

'In a way I was glad it happened. I doubt our relationship would have survived. Gaurav's family was intimidating.'

'Wish we had met when you were in London,' said Ajai.

'We have met now,' I responded.

'Things are different now,' he said softly.

6

"Match-maker, match-maker make me a match."

Woken up with a tug and pull, my mother unleashed the morning sun on my face.

Yesterday had been the most memorable day of my life and I had drifted off to a beautiful sleep once Ajai had messaged that he had boarded the flight. The sweetness of his voice, the fragrance of musk and his gentle touch had imprinted itself in every cell of my body.

Romancing and drinking and making merry in my dreams was all erased the moment my mum's loud screaming rang in my ears.

'Wake up Priya,' Mum's hoarse voice snapped me out of my reverie.

I slid my head under the pillow to escape from her loud scream. Never giving up on me, mum switched off the air-conditioning. Jolting myself out of my bed, I glided to the washroom. I glimpsed at myself while brushing. Blinking and smiling for I had fallen in love with myself. Knowing that someone loves you, makes you love yourself more.

Locking my room door, I draped the saree Ajai had gifted me. A loud knock at the door had me scream.

'I am changing, relax.'

'Hurry up Priya,' shouted mum.

Unable to drape the saree, I folded it and placed it in my cupboard.

'Priya baby, I have your dress,' said Supriya knocking on my door.

I unlocked my room door. Supriya was holding on to a yellow colored *salwar suit*. I pulled the suit from her and shut the door.

I slipped on the bangles Ajai had gifted me and walked out of my room in my Indian wear. Mum was waiting in the living room. 'See how nice you look in these clothes,' said mum.

'This is yours, isn't it?' I asked.

'Yes, but look how perfectly it fits you,' said mum 'I bought it from a designer store. It's a bit lose for me now.'

'You don't need to explain, I am used to wearing your and Sonali's hand me down.'

'Where is the *dupatta*? You cannot enter a gurudwara without it. Go get it,' said mum as we entered the lift.

Before I could step out to fetch it, Supriya appeared with the *dupatta* spread across her hands.

'You forgot to wear this baby,' said Supriya.

'Thank you Supriya. You are always so kind.' I responded as she shut the lift door.

'You are twenty seven years old Priya, you need to learn to be responsible,' demanded mum

'I only forgot the *dupatta*,' I grumbled as we entered the car.

The car halted outside the gurudwara and at that very moment my mobile buzzed.

Ajai had landed in London. *Landed. Thank you for your time. Missing you!*

I felt a tingle of excitement run up my spine and I broke into a smile only to be shaken from my reverie.

'Cover your head properly Priya,' demanded mum as we walked into the *gurudwara*.

'I know I have to cover my head mum. I am doing it,' upset with mum for not letting me enjoy the moment.

'When will you learn to talk sweetly?'

'When you will learn to treat me properly,' I responded

Upset with mother I walked into the sanctum . The granthi was reciting the Ek Onkar prayer.

"There is but one God. His name is Truth, He is the Creator. He fears none; He is without hate. He never dies, He is beyond the cycle of births and death. He is self-

illuminated. He is realized by the kindness of the True Guru. He was True in the beginning; He was True when the ages commenced and has ever been True. He is also True now."

Hoping to feel a surge of peace I shut my eyes. Instead of finding solace in the beautiful *shabd*, my mind was hopping from one thought to another. The moments that I shared with Ajai and of a possible future with him. Unable to fight my thoughts, I bowed and walked out of the *gurudwara*.

Within a few minutes mum had caught up with me as I waited by the gate.

'We could have sat longer. Why did you rush out?' asked mum.

'I wasn't comfortable,' I responded as I called for Rajan to bring the car.

'What is with you Priya? Don't you have any values?'

'What has values got to do with visiting a *gurudwara*?'

'It's a good habit to visit the *gurudwara*, it's peaceful,' said mum.

'I was not at peace in there,' I responded.

'I cannot believe it Priya, that you don't find peace in a holy place.'

'You do?' I asked.

'Yes,' said mum.

'Then why are you so nervous at home? Why do you behave so rudely with dad?' I questioned as Rajan opened the door to the car.

'I don't want to talk about it,' mum replied curtly as she slid into the car.

Mum instructed Rajan to head towards Worli.

'Why are we going to Worli?' I asked as mum dabbed her lips with gloss.

'To register you with a match maker.'

'I can find myself a partner, I don't need a match maker,' I grumbled.

'Priya I don't know which is worse, your choice of boys or your choice of shoes,' said mum looking at my mojris.

'These are a special gift.'

'From whom?'

I stayed silent.

Facing no traffic on our route to Worli we reached our destination in fifteen minutes. Striding up three floors of the dilapidated building we rang the bell to Miss Meeta Makhijani's residence.

The sound of the bell was a song from the 80's.

'How cheap is that,' I said rolling my eyes.

'Speak softly Priya, what if she hears you,' said mother.

'Please come in,' said the young girl wearing a colourful salwar kurta and braided hair.

'Isn't she underage to be working as a helper?' I whispered.

'Mind your own business Priya,' responded mum.

The eyes widened and narrowed once again as the door opened and a waft of fish filled the air. My mother placed her scarf on her nose and I placed my hand.

The helper ushered us to the small terrace cum office and handed us a form. Taking a swig from her Evian water bottle, my mother filled in the form.

NAME: PRIYA WADHWANI

SEX: FEMALE

AGE: 27 years

EDUCATION: Masters in Finance

MOTHER'S NAME: RADHIKA

FATHER'S NAME: KAMAL

SIBLINGS: SONALI MAKHIJA

HOBBIES:SWIMMING/DANCING/PAINTING/ SINGING

'That's a lie,' I interrupted, 'I neither like swimming nor dancing nor painting and nor can I sing to save my life. I only enjoy reading.'

My mum added reading and questioned, 'Should I write arguing with mum too as your hobby?'

Pulling out an old picture of mine, my mother stuck it on the form with the glue that the helper had left behind.

'That's my engagement picture. How could you use this picture?' I questioned.

Ignoring my remark my mother continued filling the form and handed it to the helper who was back with two glasses of water. After a few minutes, walked in a petite woman with salt and pepper hair, styled in a blunt.

'Hello, I am Meeta Makhijani.'

'I am Radhika Wadhwani and this is Priya,' said mum as she handed Meeta the form.

'Hello Aunty,' squeaked Meeta.

'You can call me Radhika,' mum snapped.

Meeta smirked and looked at the form.

'Priya Wadhwani?' asked Meeta as she read through the form, 'You look different in the picture,' she added.

'Sorry that was the only one we had,' said mum and continued clarifying, 'you see, Priya has just returned from London and we haven't had time to click any new pictures.'

'Of course, I can understand,' sneered Meeta.

'So you're from London,' said Meeta as she glared at me.

'Isn't that what mum just said.'

Ignoring me, Meeta steered towards mum, 'Your daughter is quite different. I can understand how stressed you must be Mrs. Wadhwani.'

'Today's generation is so difficult,' mother complained.

'Sorry to interrupt but today's generation is not difficult. The difference between the generations is that this one speaks their mind.'

Ignoring my remark, Meeta continued bantering, 'As mentioned over the phone, the charges for our service is ten thousand rupees, Mrs. Wadhwani.'

'Ten thousand rupees, for finding me a match!' I gasped.

My mother flipped at my remark, pinching me on my thigh, she whispered, 'Priya keep quiet.'

The woman examined me, as if I was a commodity and then locked eyes with my mother. 'You should have informed your daughter about my charges. I have people from all over the world registered with me. We do a lot of work here.'

'My daughter's been away for long and has lost track of how expensive Mumbai is now,' mum placated on my behalf.

'You must inform her that life in Mumbai is unlike these foreign countries where everything is easy. Ten thousand rupees is nothing for the work I do here. You can go through the files and jot down names and numbers of the boys that interest you. Please note that our job is only to give you the data, not the character information of the prospect. We are not liable if the financial status is not as the boy might have mentioned in the form. It will be your responsibility to do a complete research on the family before you plunge into the relationship.'

Her speech was as fast as the disclaimer's that they read at the end of an insurance policy.

Meeta excused herself and stepped out of the tiny office.

'How many times have I asked you to think before you speak,' Mum snapped as soon as the woman was out of sight.

'What would this woman know about match making, when she herself is a spinster.'

'Priya why are you always judging people? What has her choice of profession got to do with her marital status? She is only a mediator to connect people and I think she is doing a good job. She is very popular amongst the Sindhis.'

'I am surprised that despite being a Punjabi you wish for both your daughters to be married into Sindhi families.'

'I am a Punjabi, but the family you are born into is Sindhi.'

I believed that my mother detested dad but a realization dawned that however harsh she may be with father, my mother valued his family traditions.

'But I find this woman strange, do you believe that good families approach her. Look at her house,' I groaned.

At that very moment Meeta walked into the room.

'Let me inform you Priya Wadhwani, that I have more than a thousand names in those files. I have highly reputed families coming to me for a Mr or Ms. Right for their children.'

Then glaring at my mother Meeta continued, 'Mrs. Wadhwani, I have met many girls but none of them has been as rude as your daughter. I can assure you that it will be quite a task finding your girl a match,' seethed Meeta.

'Looks like your family too was unsuccessful in finding a match for you,' I retorted.

My mother pulled me out of the woman's house with five names penned and saved in her Michael Kors bag. Pinching me on my arm mother walked me out of Meeta's house, yelling, 'You need to change Priya. You are extremely rude and insensitive.'

'Who comes to these match makers in these modern times when a guy is easily accessible on social media,' I asked mother.

'It is for girls like you, who make wrong decisions and whose parents are forced to intervene,' mother replied, at her sarcastic best.

7

"Rejection is merely a redirection:
a course correction to your destiny"
- Bryant McGill

My mind had taken over my heart, cautioning it of the consequences of falling in love and attaching myself to a man who was all set to tie the knot. Ajai's wedding dates were finalized, and preparations had begun. Despite realizing the facts, my heart bewailed for Ajai. My body was hungry, my soul desolate, my heart skipping beats and my stomach refusing to digest. Like a cosseted child wanting a candy that he had liked, but the candy was already sold to another child. The world was unfair to average looking people.

My mother had been in a foul mood for the past two days, while I had been avoiding Ajai's messages and my sister's calls. Dad's insistence to join his work had agitated me further. Pulling out a bottle of Sula Rose from the bar cabinet, I poured myself a glass of wine as I dressed for Ritika's party. I was in no mood but Ritika never gave up on me. 'You cannot sit at home and sulk. You are coming for the party and I will not take "no" for an answer,' Ritika had pleaded over the phone.

'Don't sulk for a guy who is unable to stand up for love. If he is not standing up now he would never stand up after marriage. You don't need a man who is tied to his mother's apron. Priya, always settle for a guy who will love you more than you love him,' Ritika had reprimanded when she heard my sob story.

Slipping into a long black off shoulder gown and consuming the entire bottle of Sula, I headed to my friend Ritika's bash at her bungalow in Juhu.

Ritika and I were club friends, friends that bonded while playing squash. An athlete by nature, Ritika won every championship that the club sponsored. A slender body, silky hair and a gait that had many heads turn when she walked into the club. Many boys started playing squash just to hang around her. But Ritika chose a middle-class struggling actor, Rajiv Khanna.

Eloping with Rajiv Khanna had her parents infuriated for a few years, but once Rajiv attained stardom, Ritika was accepted by all the family members with open arms. Rajiv's success lasted for a few years, followed by his accidental death.

Rajiv was found dead in his bath tub while Ritika and I were enjoying our girls holiday in Spain. Rajiv's sudden death raised many questions and all fingers pointed at Ritika. But Ritika had enough of her own wealth to kill the man she loved. Nit picking on other's life is a common human trait and Ritika tried hard to ignore the gossip mills. But within a few months of struggling with depression, Ritika broke away from the clutches of sorrow and evolved as a compassionate and helpful human being.

'Hi Priya. No response. Hope all ok,' read Ajai's message as our car moved at a snail's pace towards Ritika's home. Within a few seconds another message read, 'My mother is in Goa and has fixed the wedding for the eighth December. You have to be there.'

I could not resist responding, 'Sorry will not be able to make it.'

Ajai called me as soon as I declined the invitation.

'Please, don't say no,' the words spilled out of his mouth as soon as I answered his call.

'I don't know Ajai, it's a busy time.'

'Please it will make me happy,' Ajai insisted.

My heart melted hearing him plead. I could not resist responding with a yes.

'Thank you so much Priya,' gushed Ajai.

'Are you out?' he asked.

'Yes, going for a friend's party.'

'I am sorry then to disturb you. Will chat soon.'

My last hope of ever being with Ajai was crumbling. The wedding was fixed, there was no chance that we would ever be together. A battle was waging within. A struggle to erase Ajai from my memory forever.

Another beep, this time the message was from mum. 'Don't keep the driver too long. Tomorrow morning is my rotary club meeting at 10:00 am.'

From being an independent woman, I had become dependent on my parents for my survival.

If only I could find myself a good job as I was not keen on working with dad. Dad was a difficult man and spending ten hours with him would drain me of my energy.

No responses were coming in from the companies I had applied to. Unable to hop onto a train, I was looking for jobs closer to home. We finally arrived at our destination. Scents of jasmine and tuberose filled the air. A life size picture of Rajiv placed on a large altar at the entrance was decorated with colourful flowers. Ritika had never stopped loving Rajiv and continued celebrating his birth anniversary every year.

Ritika had paid a price for her husband's addictive habits. The world had no idea that Rajiv had died in the bath-tub because of an overdose of cocaine. It did not matter what people said about Ritika but she protected him even after his death, at the cost of her own reputation.

Wearing a long white flowy dress with hair tied up in a loose bun, Ritika exuded an air of elegance as she greeted every guest with a warm hug. She was a mix of impishness and maturity. Her warm hug brought consolation to my agitated mind.

'I am so glad you came,' said Ritika as she pulled me towards the bar and ordered two shots.

'To Rajiv and to our friendship,' gushed Ritika.

We clinked our glasses, 'arriba, abajo, al centro y pa dentro.' A phrase we learnt in Spain on our visit to Malaga. A holiday where we giggled, shopped souvenirs, visited Picasso's museum and explored the bars in the old town of Marbella. That's where Ritika had received a call of her husband's death.

With a bitter taste in our mouths, Ritika queried about my crush for Ajai.

'It is not a crush,' I squeaked, 'It is love.'

Ritika simpered as I expressed my emotions for Ajai, breaking into a warm hug again.

'Let him go Priya. I am sure, you will find someone better. Someone who will love you, respect you and care about your feelings.'

Pulling myself away I murmured, 'I don't know if I am as lucky as you.'

'How am I lucky Priya?' whispered Ritika. 'I lost the man who loved me the most in this world.'

'To Rajiv,' I cheered as we downed another shot.

'Now let me attend to other guests, Priya. You make

yourself comfortable. I will be back to check on you,' said Ritika.

Ritika's guests were an eclectic mixture of celebrities, strugglers and common people.

With nothing much to do, I checked on Ajai's messages as I downed a couple of shots.

Feeling light headed and dizzy, I headed to the beach for fresh air. The soft touch of moonlight caressed my warm skin while the salty breeze moistened my lips. I watched the waves as they playfully wet the sand and slipped back into the ocean .

The calm sea, the twinkling stars and the stillness, triggered sweet memories of the moments I spent with Ajai. My senses were awakened and lust was gently gripping me.

And then suddenly I heard a hoarse voice.

'Hi! I am Malik,' said a middle-aged burly man. I looked at the man who stood beside me with a cigar in his hand.

'I am Priya,' I slurred.

'What are you doing out here?' asked Malik.

'Enjoying the breeze,' I slumped on the sand. The slit in my gown exhibited my cellulite ridden thighs.

'Aren't you enjoying the party?' he asked.

'Needed fresh air.'

I gulped the cocktail I had brought along.

Malik plonked himself beside me and offered me a puff. I held the stogie in my mouth and inhaled letting out a deep cough.

Malik pulled the cigar from my hand and patted my back.

'One does not inhale a cigar, you need to hold on to the smoke in the mouth and enjoy the flavour,' said Malik.

I followed Malik's instructions and after a few puffs , I got the hang of it.

Malik gently slid his hand through my gown, caressing my thighs. My knotted stomach and yearning body did not reject, the touch of a stranger. I gently shut my eyes and visualized Ajai. The gentle kisses turned into violent smooching, my body tingling with ecstasy. Believing the man to be Ajai, my mind was playing games as my body gave in to temptation.

8

"Akhar parh alif jo,warq sabh wisaar;
Andar Too'n Ujaar, Pana Parhanden Ketra"
"Read letter A(Alif), forget all other pages, cleanse your
heart, how long can you read pages and pages?"
- Shah Abdul Latif

Lilaram Wadhwani, my grand-father was forced out of his homeland Sindh, in the year 1947 when along with his parents and three sisters he crossed the new border to settle in unfamiliar lands.

Homeless and penniless, yet determined to live with dignity grandfather arrived in Mumbai to make a living while his family took refuge in Jaipur. Within a few years of working with a garment manufacturer Lilaram Wadhwani started his own small factory and married Kheemi; my grandmother who was only seventeen then. Kamal, my dad was the only child that survived, after three miscarriages.

Within two years of Sonali's birth, grandmother passed away due to cancer. After granny's death, grandfather found solace in the durbar and strived hard to keep Sindhi culture alive by organizing Sindhi programmes.

Our bedtime stories with grandfather were of his times spent in Sindh. Names of Prof. Ram Panjwani, Bhagwanti Nawani, Bhagat Kanwaram and Sufi saint Shah Abdul Latif were often mentioned in the conversations between him and the late Master of the Manjhad durbar. While the Master would converse with us in Sindhi, we would respond in Hindi or English. As we grew older the visits were infrequent and once grand-father died the visits came to an end. An occasional phone call to the Master was all we did to keep in touch.

Since the time I returned from Ritika's home, my whole body was squirming with uneasiness and my head was pounding. A feeling of loneliness and dejection was setting in. I had three missed calls from Ritika and two from my sister but I was in no mood to answer. Thankfully mum had left early morning for her charity work to a village close by and dad had left for work.

With no clue where I was headed, I slipped into the yellow *salwar suit* that hung in my bathroom.

After walking aimlessly for a while, I headed to the durbar where grandfather spent most of his time.

In the midst of the hustle bustle of the market, was a white building that read the name Manjhand Durbar. The building had been revamped from the time I had last visited. The space where grandfather stood behind a table to safely keep the slippers of devotees had been transformed into shoe racks with numbers. I left my slippers in the rack and walked up the marbled staircase that led to the sanctum. The sanctum where grandfather would join the choir to sing the praises of Lord Jhulelal on Cheti Chand that was the Sindhi New Year. That was the only time mum and dad too would step into the durbar. Few monks sat still in meditation, while others prepared the paraphernalia of the evening aarti.

Bowing to the many deities and saints, I headed to the room where Master met those who came to meet him and seek his guidance.

Dressed in an orange robe, Master Gobindji was sitting on the floor, his hair loosely tied in a bun as he conversed with a young scrawny man. Acknowledging my presence with his merciful eyes.

'Temptation comes as a passer-by. It knocks on the door of your heart and wishes to be admitted as a guest. Beware of this guest for if you allow him in, it will stay as a Master.' Master sermoned the stubbled man.

'Please bless me so I can forego my vices Master. Please...' his frail voice trailed.

A victim to alcohol addiction, I guessed. His side profile revealing bags under his eyes.

My stomach that had been in a peculiar rebellion had subdued in the presence of the Master.

Master's face beamed with serenity, as he spoke, 'keep

away from bad company and chant the name of the Lord.'

'Help me come out of this vice,' said the lanky man.

'I can only guide and bless you have to help yourself.' said the Master.

'Go and sit for a while in the sanctum. You will find strength to overcome your weakness,' said the Master. As soon as the young man left, I crawled towards the master.

'Nice to see you after so long Priya. How have you been?'

I bowed in reverence tears trickling down my cheeks. I had no idea if it was the guilt that was surfacing or the fact that I had not visited the Master since grandfather's death.

I discreetly wiped my tears with the corner of my dupatta.

'Are you back in Mumbai?' asked the Master.

'Yes,' I responded, 'Mum and dad wanted me return home. So I was left with no choice but to comply with their wishes,' my eyes gazing at Master's feet.

'And are you happy to be home?' he asked.

'I don't know. It's not easy living with them, specially mother. There is a constant disagreement between us. I don't know how long I can survive with them,' I responded.

'The disagreement, is nothing but an internal battle of the *gunas*. The conflict is between good and evil intentions and the pure and impure thoughts that arise within us. In the Bhagavad Gita, Lord Krishna describes our body as the field and self as the knower of the field. You are battling not with anyone outside but with those strong sanskaras that you are born with.'

'How can I erase my bad *sanskaras*? They don't leave me.'

'Firstly, by avoiding any kind of intoxicants. They pull you away from from living a moral life and make you a slave of the habit.'

How did the Master know so much about my life. Did he know about last night too. Was he watching my thoughts?

'To erase habits is not so easy, specially if you say we are born with them.' I responded

'You are right. You say so because your mind wants you to believe so. Your mind wants to control you, keep you as its slave for ever. If you do not control your mind your old habit patterns will keep taking you back to performing actions that it is habituated to. Train your mind to control the ten weaknesses that are critical in the downfall of the human race. Greed, Lust, Anger, Attachment, Arrogance, Jealousy, Slander, Laziness, Fear and Hatred.'

The loud sound of the conch signalled that it was time for the evening *aarti*.

Master stood up to the sound of the conch, 'The removal of character defects is a constant challenge and only by strengthening your character can you control your weakness and the temptations that arise within you. Your grandfather, Lilaram was a man of values and lived a pious life. He loved you more than anyone else in this world,' the Master lit the aarti as he spoke.

Holding the silver plate lit with camphor, he rotated the aarti in obeisance to the Gods, goddesses and saints. The lyrics of the aarti were ingrained in my mind as I visited the sanctum often as a child.

Standing in silence I prayed for grandfather's guidance. My eyes brimming with tears, as I thought of the times I spent with grandfather. One of the moments was of my eighteenth birthday when grandfather had gifted me the Bhagavad Gita. 'Priya this book will help you sail through life's various twists and turns. Whenever you feel lost, read it and you will find your answers.'

9

"All differences in this world are of degree and not of kind because oneness is the secret of everything."
- Swami Vivekananda

I ransacked my drawers and cupboards to find the sacred book that grandfather had gifted me. Unable to unearth the treasure, I stormed into my mother's bedroom to find her busy conversing on the her phone and posting pictures on facebook. I was asked to leave in a sweet tone, 'Priya beta, I am on the phone,' the tone that she used when she was in conversation with her high society friends.

No response from mum had me raid the guest room that was earlier my grand father's room. I realized that mum had erased every memory of his from that room. It saddened me to think of how easily we forget the ones who brought us to this earth. I wondered if dad ever missed his father.

Giving up hope, I let Supriya get back to her routine, lest mother get annoyed with her. Grabbing my Marlboro packet, I headed to the terrace. Grey clouds were collecting in the sky, ready to shower the city. While igniting the lighter, a thought crossed my mind and I left the cigarette along with the lighter on the small stool sprinting towards the bed.

Pulling up the mattress, I lifted the wooden plank with one hand. Below my mattress and the plank lay piles of books, papers and my school diaries. With one hand holding on to the plank, I scrambled through the heap of books. There they were, two volumes of the Bhagavad Gita, 'God talks with Arjuna.'

I flipped the pages of Volume 1 and randomly selected a page. *Conquering the two-sided passion, desire and anger. Chapter 3- Verse 36.*

Few lines that were underlined by my grand-father caught my attention-

"Every man sometimes experiences a peculiar state, even as he strives towards virtuous action, he seems to be dragged into temptation, almost by force."

"Bad habits of past lives appear as strong moods and octopus-like inclinations whose tentacles are strengthened by evil company and thoughtless actions."

I promised myself to read a page every day from this sacred book that was close to grandfather's heart. I had watched him spend his mornings reading from the book and underlining pages and at times making notes.

While my hunt for peace had begun, mum was driven by the desire of power and fame. New relationships were founded, old friends were now being avoided. Aunty Gayatri had been mum's best friend till we graduated from school.

In grade seven, I had a huge crush on aunty Gayatri's son Rohit. Short and round like his mother Rohit was a nerd who was disinterested in girls so, I moved on. A call to aunty Gayatri meant that mum needed something from Crawford market and had no time to shop. And aunty Gayatri more often then not complied to my mother's demands..

'Gayatri you can leave. I have things to do now. And thank you so much for helping me out,' said mum as she instructed the decorators to straighten the vase of orchids. Aunty Gayatri walked away disheartened but my mum did not wince even once nor did she feel guilty.

'How is Rohit?' I inquired.

'He is good, living with his boyfriend in town,' she responded sheepishly.

'You must be lonely without him,' I asked.

'No, I am glad he is not living with us. It's difficult to explain people that he is not normal,' said Gayatri.

'But it's normal aunty. If he prefers boys, it's his choice. We are living in a modern society and gay marriages are acceptable.'

'I don't understand your generation Priya,' said Gayatri as she entered the lift.

A high tea at our home meant that our kitchen was raided by caterers and our living room by decorators. Unable to bear the commotion at home, I headed to the club to meet Ritika.

'So tell me, who's this new friend your mother is wooing?' asked Ritika.

'Pavan Ahuja and her sister Riddhima Mehra,' I rattled. 'My mother is obsessed with her new friends.'

'Your mother is impressive. We have to give it to her, she has managed to move around with the crème de la crème of the society.'

'I despise the way she treats aunty Gayatri. And that woman complies with her commands. I don't think she cares about anyone except her social standing. I wonder if she cares for me,' I contemplated.

'She does care for you Priya. Your mother enjoys social stimulation,' added Ritika. 'Anyways, do you know anything about her latest friend, Pavan Ahuja?'

'No. what is her story?'

'That woman is twice divorced and lives off the alimony she receives from her ex-husbands. It's rumoured that she is a mistress to one of the top politicians of our country,' said Ritika, a mischief glint in her eyes.

'Do you think mum knows all this?' I asked baffled.

'She should, everyone in society does. And your mum wants to befriend her hoping to be invited to the much talked about wedding in town. wedding of Riddhima's daughter. Riddhima is the wife of one of the most influential builders of the city. The interesting part is that he has a wife and daughter at home and a mistress in the same building.'

'Doesn't his wife know?' I asked in disbelief.

'Obviously she knows about it. Most of the men in this city have mistresses, and their wives know about it but they prefer to turn a blind eye.'

'Why?'

'The husbands are paying for their bills. There are rumours that Pavan's brother-in-law' pays for her expenses too.'

'Pavan gets alimony, has a politician boyfriend and a brother-in-law paying her bills. 'What the hell is happening with these older people? And they curse our generation.' I grumbled. 'Mum wants to befriend these women, while she ignores and demeans genuine friends like aunty Gayatri.'

The city gossip had my head reeling. I felt less guilty. If married men and women had no morals, then why ridicule unmarried women.

'This will be the grandest wedding the city has seen. The Mehra's and the Rao's and Pavan is her bait. Don't you see it Priya? Your mother is a true Mumbai socialite,' said Ritika.

Moving from Mumbai social scene, our conversation moved to the Bhagavad Gita.

Impressed with the fact that I had begun reading the Bhagavad Gita, she said, 'I had no idea you were spiritual,' as she sipped her cappuccino, wiping the froth on her lips, with a tissue. 'Twice a year I go for

Vipassana,' she added looking smug.

Confused with the word I probed Ritika to explain me the same in depth.

'Vipassana helps in self-transformation through self-observation. I spend ten days in silence and eat only two meals a day. Ten hours of meditation every day helps develop a healthy mind.'

'And a hungry stomach.'

'It's not that bad Priya. I suggest you try it once in your life. It will help you connect to yourself.'

'I am not ready as yet Ritika. I cannot imagine myself sitting in silence. Maybe when I am older.'

'Priya, wisdom does not come with age but with the yearning to grow and learn.'

'Maybe one day. Not for now I have just begun reading the Bhagavad Gita, which my grandfather had gifted me, and I think that is a good beginning,' I declared.

'It's a good start to changing yourself,' remarked Ritika, 'but that change has to be consistent.'

'Am I that bad Ritika?' I asked

'Why do you think that you are bad. We all have some good and some bad qualities. All we need to do is to be aware of our bad qualities and work on them,' responded Ritika.

'I have quite a few bad qualities and one of them is my inability to control the temptations of physical closeness.'

Ritika listened silently, her eyes fixated on me as she held her cup of tea.

'At your party the other night I gave in to the temptation. My weak moment and that too with a married man by the name of Malik.'

On hearing my episode with Malik, Ritika dropped her cappuccino on her lucknowi white kurta.

I helped her wipe out the stain.

'That man is as old as your father. How could you?,' Ritika demanded.

'I know. I tracked him on facebook.'

'One should not drink so much that they are unable to control their senses,' sighed Ritika.

'I went to the durbar to seek forgiveness.'

'And you believe you are forgiven?'

'It's the *sanskaras* I am born with from my previous births. I am working on them.'

'We are not teenagers anymore Priya we need to take control of ourselves and move towards the path that will bring true joy. It's good to have fun but not at the cost of morality,' said Ritika

'You are right, Ritika.'

'And what about Ajai?'

'He is a friend,' I responded.

'Friend with benefit?' asked Ritika.

'No, not at all,' admiring Ritika's Jimmy Choo nude pumps.

******

Within two weeks time, Ritika's prediction had come true when the invite to the Mehra wedding arrived at our home.

Mum travelled to Dubai with Pavan for a collagen facial.

'Why can't you live a normal simple life? We are not millionaires like them. I cannot cope up with your expenses,' Dad howled as soon as mum returned from Dubai with her face puffed up and lip movement restricted.

'You have used the credit card above the spending limit,' he yelled.

'Don't you have any shame, I have just arrived and this is how you greet me,' this time mother's voice was louder. 'I need to get Priya married into a wealthy family and for that I have to move with good family women.'

'Being wealthy does not mean that they are good family women. Everyone knows what reputation Pavan has in this city. I forbade you to go and yet you went to Dubai with her for a collagen facial,' whined dad.

'You have no class Kamal; how can you talk about my

friend in this manner. You have no friends, which is why you are jealous. I am not sleeping around and cheating on you as you did.'

Mum stormed out of the room while I tried to process what mum had just said.

Dad gasped in shock sinking into the chair on my terrace. Dad composed himself and asked for a light.

'You are not supposed to be smoking dad.'

'I rather die than live a life of misery.'

'You and mum should sort out your differences. You two have drifted too far apart,' unable to question mother's remark on his cheating her.

'Yes, we have. And I don't blame her for her attitude towards me. I am the culprit of this broken marriage.'

Dad inhaled and exhaled a few puffs before he spoke.

'What's the matter dad, is there something I don't know?'

'It's all my fault, I broke Radhika's trust.'

'Radhika and I were at the lowest phase in our relationship after you left for Uni to London. We were going through a mid life crisis. During that time, I had appointed a new secretary Julia. She was young, talented and hardworking. Julia was like a breath of fresh air in my life and as a man would I was attracted to her and her free spirited nature. We spent many hours talking about politics, nature, music during office hours. We then began meeting after office hours.'

My heart was sinking as dad continued, 'Our relationship had transformed from employer/employee to friends and then to lovers.'

I felt disgusted with my dad at that moment. I wanted to dig a grave and sleep in it forever. My dad who had no time for us when we were growing up had spent days and nights with a stranger. He had not only betrayed our mother's trust but also his daughters.

'How did mother find out?' I asked

'I had lied about traveling to Delhi for work, when your mother saw Julia and me at a night club she was visiting with friends,' said dad.

I could imagine the pain and shock that mum would have experienced on finding dad with a younger woman and that too with her friends around.

'It's shameful, all this is ridiculously shameful,' I recoiled on the floor and wept bitterly.

Dad held my face and sobbed, 'I made a mistake.'

'How could you berate mum in this manner? How could you not have thought of your children?'

'Taking control of temptations is not easy, I got carried away and realized my mistake that night.'

'You needed mum to catch you red-handed to realize your mistake. Please dad! You would have left us for that home breaker.'

'I would never have done that, Priya. My ability to think was clouded by lust,' said dad.

I empathized with my mum and thought of how giving she had been. She could have walked out of the house, but she stuck on for our future. Mum had forgiven dad but not forgotten that he had betrayed her trust. Dad was trying hard to earn back mum's love and respect. While mum's resentment had turned into balls of fire that she volleyed at dad. As its rightly said, trust takes years to build, seconds to break and forever to repair.

Dad's and mum's relationship was a work in progress.

'I want you all to forgive me,' cried dad.

'I am no one to forgive you dad, it is mum who needs to erase the pain.'

'How?' said dad.

'Make her feel loved and wanted.'

'I try to but it's not easy for me. I am not an expressive person Priya.'

'You don't need words to express your love, do it with actions.'

Stubbing the butt on the parapet, dad walked towards me, 'I love you all. You are my family my life,' said dad as he embraced me.

10

*"What counts in making a happy marriage is not
so much as how compatible you are,
how you deal with incompatibility" - Leo Tolstoy*

While I watched my mother being draped in a Tarun Tahiliani saree, I felt protective towards her. Her silence towards dad's wrong doing was her way of protecting us.

I kissed my mum's hand as she looked at her reflection in the mirror.

'You are so beautiful mum.'

Mum blushed and asked me to click a picture. If the likes on facebook made her happy, then why not. Within me there were feelings of guilt that had been surfacing since dad confessed his betrayal. I had been extremely judgmental about mother's obsession with herself. But that was her way of coping with rejection.

Dad and mum were deeply in love when they met each other. Unable to persuade their parents to accept their relation they had eloped and got married. Mum believed dad was her Mr.Right, till he betrayed her trust.

I prayed that mum would be able to heal and dad would walk that extra mile to help her heal faster.

'Priya is looking nice.' Vaibhavi our hairdresser stated, as she brushed the few frizzy strands that refused to be tamed. Mum was pleased with my hair and make-up but fussed on the choice of my saree. She wanted me to wear one of Sonali's designer saree, which I blatantly refused. I did not wish to upset mum but Ajai had insisted that I wear the saree he gifted me, for the Mehra's engagement party.

'How am I looking dad?' I asked dad who was sitting in the living room watching the news. The loud screams from the television had the anchor, debating on a menial statement made by a politician. The panel that consisted of eminent personalities were yelling their lungs out, struggling to be heard on national news and in the process making a fool of themselves.

Dad turned his eyes towards me and stood up with his arms stretched out. 'The saree suits you Priya. You look lovely.'

'You too are looking gorgeous Radhika,' said dad as mum walked into the living room.

'Since when have you started complimenting me?' she eyed him quizzically.

'You are the most beautiful woman in this world,' said dad.

'Mum accept the compliment with grace.'

'Okay. Thank you. Priya let's go now,' groaned mum.

The moment Sonali entered the car, mum complimented her for her expensive saree and then turned to me. 'That's a Sabyasachi Sonali is wearing, look how beautiful it is.'

'Priya is looking nice too mum. I like her saree,' responded Sonali 'Which designer is it?'

'Santacruz market,' hissed mum.

'You know it is from the market that is why you are criticising it, if I had told you I got it from Tarun Tahiliani you would have praised it. Mum, it's not the price that matters, it's your confidence that does.'

'How can you be confident wearing a cheap saree?'

'I can, mum. I don't need a price tag to define me,' I added.

'Leave it na, you two,' Sonali pleaded.

After a round of ten to fifteen pictures at the photo op, we headed to the banquet hall. Walking through the floral sculptures of elephants and fragrance of peonies and roses that filled the passage way we entered the main hall. A hash tag of the couple was illustrated with white lilies.

'What a waste of money,' I said in disgust.

'If you have it, flaunt it,' said Sonali.

'Priya you are too negative about everything,' said mum and 'we are their guests. We should respect the fact that we were invited. You cannot slice someone at their own party.'

'You'll are not bitching because this is a rich man's wedding. Otherwise by now, you would have criticized every stem and flower that is around here.

'Priya, you are such a negative Nancy,' exclaimed Sonali.

'Can we head to the bar, instead of loitering around the entrance?' I demanded.

'This is where you will have the best glimpse of stars and celebrities,' said mum.

'Are you here for them or for your friend, Pavan?' I asked.

'Priya why can't you ever enjoy, instead of behaving like a wet blanket,' complained Sonali.

'Why would you want to click pictures with them? They are not your friends,' I asked.

'It gives me a thrill. The more pictures you post with important people, the more importance you get. People believe that you mingle with them,' responded mum

'I don't understand that theory,' I responded. 'You are just clicking a picture like a fan. That is not something to be proud about.'

'But people don't know that. You want to make them believe that you are friends with them,' said mum.

Adults had lost it, I thought to myself. *Technology had robbed them of their sanity. Instead of aging with grace, they were behaving like teenagers*

I stood by the bar and ordered a martini for myself. A whatsapp video call from Ajai had me excited. I had sent him a picture of myself in the saree he had gifted me.

'You look lovely in the saree,' said Ajai. The view of Hyde park bringing back memories of London.

'Thank you, for this beautiful gift,' I blushed.

Holding the phone further I twirled to the side, for Ajai to have a glimpse. But the call dropped and unable to connect again, I picked up my drink from the bar and headed outdoors for a smoke.

On the open terrace of the ballroom were scattered young and old people. I walked towards a beefy ponytailed man who was resting against the wooden pillar with his one foot on the parapet, a cigarette smouldering between his fingers.

'Could I borrow a cigarette?' I asked.

'Of course, beautiful,' he exclaimed sliding his hand into his trouser pocket. Extending the packet towards me. I pulled out one cigarette and slid it between my lips. The man drew closer and lit the cigarette. The scent of an expensive cologne filled my nostrils and I sneezed.

'Nice perfume,' I smiled

'Gucci bloom,' said the man. 'I am Samar Malkani and you are?'

'Priya Wadhwani,' I exhaled before announcing my name.

'And are you here from the boy's or girl's side?' asked Samar, picking up his glass of whiskey from the parapet.

'None, I don't know anyone here.'

Samar laughed, 'That makes two of us.'

'Gate crasher?' I asked.

'Some far of cousin to wife,' he sniggered.

'Family then?' I probed.

'There is no family concept in Mumbai,' said Samar.

'I thought we Indians were attached to our families.'

'Once upon a time, not any more. Our priorities have changed. The most distant relations are with family members.' said Samar.

'Relationships are complicated, no doubt but cynicism leads to depression.'

'Depression is for those who are unable to face reality.'

'Everybody's perspective is different I guess.'

'Married?' he asked.

'No, not as yet,' I responded.

'No intentions to get married?' asked Samar.

'I have not yet found my Mr.Right.'

'You never will. There is no one right for anyone. It's just a farce. The perfect husband, the perfect wife. Marriage is a relationship in which one person is always right and the other is the husband.'

I answered my mother's call, as I tittered at Samar's statement.

'Why are you giggling? Hope you have not had too much to drink? Where are you? I need to introduce you to Pavan,' whispered mum, 'come to the hall, we are standing beside the entrance with Pavan.'

I stubbed my cigarette and excused myself.

As I walked past, I watched a tall slender woman in a black shimmery gown walking towards Samar. *Lucky Samar*, I thought, *or unlucky?* Was my second thought. *Not all that seems beautiful is reality.*

Beside my mother was a chiseled face woman, alarmingly bewitching.

'Priya, meet my friend, Pavan,' said mother.

'Hello aunty,' I greeted.

'You can call me Pavan,' her face breaking into deep dimples as she introduced herself.

'Pavan, find her a good match please,' pleaded mum.

'Don't worry Radhika.' said Pavan her eyes surveying me as she spoke,' I will surely be on the look out. However, I would suggest she lose a little weight. Boys want slim, sexy looking girls.'

'I am working on her diet. She was in London and you know how it is, when you have no one to cook you end up eating all junk food,' mum justifying to Pavan, as if I was answerable to people for my food habits.

'There are no excuses for not looking after oneself, you should take her to a nutritionist, enroll her in a gymnasium and take her to a dermatologist for skin whitening,' suggested Pavan.

'You are right Pavan,' said mum. The two women discussed me as if I was some kind of commodity.

'Once she has lost weight and is fairer then we can introduce her to good looking wealthy guys,' grinned Pavan.

'Thank you but I don't need anyone to find me a match. If marriage was the solution you wouldn't have divorced two husbands,' my snide remark went unheard by Pavan as she had glided away to the loud sound of drums heralding the arrival of the to be bride and groom.

'How can you make such a statement?' mother said angrily.

'How could you berate your daughter to a stranger?' I retorted.

Mum and Sonali meandered their way through the swarm of people applauding for the, to be bride and groom. Samar was right, friends come before family.

I headed to the bar and ordered for myself an apple martini as I checked my phone. Ajai's message read, 'How is the party going?'

'Shitty people, shitty party, shitty family,' I texted back.

'Will chat with you tomorrow, till then stay calm,' Ajai texted.

'Mobile phones are devils that are destroying our peace of mind,' said Samar. 'I rather spend time with my mobile than my family.'

Ordering ourselves another round of drinks, Samar and I clinked our glasses while the guest cheered for the couple.

The to be bride whose name I struggled to recollect, walked hand in hand with her beau towards the stage that was densely packed with strings of frothy flowers.

'A good business deal,' said Samar, 'An ex-politician's son and a builder's daughter.'

'What a waste of wealth. Look at all those guests lining up for attention. Bloody suckers,' I gulped yet another martini and asked for one more.

'Someone is ticked off.'

'I am livid. Look at my family, that's my sister and mother,' who were grinning at the camera that was projecting their images on the large screens that were placed in every corner of the large hall.

'You are a good looking family,' said Samar.

'They are good looking, I am the odd one.'

'Says who?' asked Samar.

'That bitch, Pavan. Can you believe it that my family stood silently, whilst she humiliated me.'

The couple had taken center stage and were waltzing to a romantic number. All eyes were glued to the couple, I looked away ordering myself another martini.

Families and friends joined the couple on stage to peppy Bollywood numbers. Carried away by the music, I climbed onto a chair and up the bar.

Next minute; Black out.

11

"The life of the dead is placed in the memory of the living"
- Marcus Cicero

The atmosphere in the room was solemn as we sat around the corpse of Chandra Kewalramani, Sonali's mother-in-law. The bump on the back of my head was tender and had me squirm on the floor. I limped towards the chair beside mum, who had not uttered a word since last night.

Mum sat solemn, but little did the world know that her solemnity arose not from Chandra's death, but from was her daughter's disgraceful behaviour. Pictures of me falling off the bar of falling off the bar chair and onto the floor had gone viral. I had no idea how, but they did.

The doctor on duty at the hospital had administered four stitches on the back of my head and sent me home only to receive a call from Vinodji.

While I had fallen from a bar chair and bumped my head, Chandra had fallen in her bathroom and died of brain haemorrhage. While I was lucky enough to be surrounded by people, Chandra had died without being discovered till late morning. Beside her, slept her husband Ram Kewalramani, who suffered from dementia and was unaware of his wife's absence in the room. The nurse that looked after Ram Kewalramani, had been dozing on the sofa of the bedroom, till Ram had asked for tea.

My eyes were teary, not for the corpse but the shooting pain in my head. Chandra's constant jibes rang in my ears, 'Are these two really sisters? And if they are, how come Priya is so dark?'

How could I feel emotional pain for a woman who had demeaned me throughout her life.

The shabd played in the background, explaining the immortality of the soul. Reminding us all that it's the body that disintegrates.

I stared at my mum's collagen facial, botoxed lips and hair. Radhika Wadhwani had spent a bomb on her face. While her friends were enjoying themselves at the mehendi celebrations of the most talked about wedding in town, mum was complying with her family obligation.

Sonali dressed in a stark white suit was running around organizing the paraphernalia for the rituals. Vinodji walked into the room in a white kurta pyjama, His eyes swollen from crying.

Everyone in the room greeted Vinodji with an embrace.

As other family members began trickling, the silent whispering had commenced.

'Why was Chandra alone? Where was Sonali at that time? Why was she not attentive of her mother-in-law?' Everyone's time to leave their body is predestined but the world wanted to blame someone and that someone would be my sister.

Sonali's absence at the time of Chandra's death was a good reason to condemn her for enjoying her life while her in-laws stayed at home.

The last person to arrive at the scene was none other than Chandra's daughter, Karishma with her husband Madhav from Bangalore. Dressed in a stark white trouser and shirt, Karishma walked into the room and fell on her mother's chest wailing and screaming.

'How could you go like this maa? If I had been here, this would never have happened.'

Hearing her loud cries, the family members broke into a whimper. Vinodji sat quietly beside the corpse.

Karishma's husband Madhav too fell on the corpse feet and wailed loudly.

'Mummyji, how could you have left us like this. I am sure someone has tried to kill you.' The statement had everyone's eyes widen up and the living room was filled with whispers once again.

'What is this man saying? Is he out of his mind,' mum groaned.

Karishma and Madhav held on to each other and wailed louder and louder.

The extreme wailing and moaning had me queasy, reminding me of the soaps that mother watched on television. Sonali approached Karishma and tried to embrace her but Karishma snubbed Sonali.

'What an eccentric woman, shouldn't she be mourning her mother's death instead of creating a scene,' I whispered.

'Her intention is to put Sonali in a spot. That girl is a witch,' said mother as Karishma continued wailing and thumping her chest.

'You killed my mother. You never did your duties and never cared for my mother.' The allegations were making me upset and I stood up and walked towards Sonali and held her hand.

'You have no right to talk to my sister in this manner. Sonali is a good daughter-in-law, a good wife and a loving mother. Why are you blaming her for your mother's death? Death is predestined, go fight with Yama. Leave my sister alone.'

Karishma's flushed red as she raised her third finger and ordered me, 'Get out of my house.' 'This is my sister's home,' I responded 'I will not leave.'

Karishma stared at me with her almond shaped eyes, 'Mind your own business,' she screamed.

The priest intervened, 'I request you both to please show some respect for the departed soul and allow me to commence the rituals.'

Snubbing me, Karishma sat beside the priest. 'Thank you Priya,' said mother smiling faintly and holding my hand.

'Death is the moment, when the soul leaves the body for its onward journey. It's not the end, but a new beginning. For seven days, the soul hangs around its familiar environment and then moves into a tunnel, as life flashes around. Excessive wailing and grief are hurdles in its journey, so please pray instead of crying, pray for her peace.' The *pandit* concluded the prayer with soothing words from the Bhagavad Gita. Words which were unable to cut through the hatred that filled the air.

Smashing an earthen diya, the body was carried to the cremation ground.

Everyone followed the body, while I slipped into a rickshaw and headed home. On the way I called Ritika, who was in a meeting. I needed to share my pain and the drama that I had witnessed, so I called Ajai.

'This is a prequel to the climax. There is an agenda behind Karishma's behaviour. She is after Vinodji's money and inheritance,' said Ajai.

'You think so?' I asked.

'Wait and watch,' responded Ajai.

12

"Materialism is the only form of distraction from true bliss"
- Douglas Horton

Chandra Kewalramani's soul had moved on but not without rousing a dispute in the Kewalramani family.

Chandra had gifted all of her jewelery and her properties to her daughter in her will. Ram Kewlaramani had gifted his daughter the home Sonali and Vinodji resided in with their children and fifty percent shares in the business that Vinodji had been running for the past ten years. Vinodji suffered in silence on hearing the news of his parents' unfairness.

'The silent one is always considered the culprit,' said mother. 'You need to speak up and file a case,' said dad.

A broken home is a breeding ground for those waiting to pick the morsels and tear it apart. The Kewalramani's were proving themselves to be quite the hawks and vultures.

Vinodji had a mild heart attack and was hospitalized for two days. On the twelfth day, Vinodji sat in the prayer meet of his mother's passing without any feelings of anger or hatred towards her or his father and sister. His sister had sent him a court notice to vacate her house in a week's time.

Sonali was refused the honor of sitting with the family, to accept condolences from friends and extended families. Without raising an eyebrow or creating a scene, Sonali walked towards the end of the hall sitting in a corner along with outsiders. Mum and I stood up from our seats and joined Sonali. I held her hand.

While everyone sat in silence mourning the loss of Chandra, my mind replayed the moments that I had spent with the woman whose death we were mourning. There was not one happy memory of her.

We stepped out of the hall to escape being shamed by the community while the person who should have been ashamed of her behavior was accepting condolences.

'Sonali I will not allow this girl to treat you in this manner. We must leave now,' coaxed mother.

'No mother, I will not leave the premises, my husband is inside and this is his mother's prayer meet. Karishma can behave the way she wants to but I will not hurt my husband's feelings,' said Sonali.

'If your husband had any respect for us, he would have been standing here with us. I cannot take this humiliation. We must leave now.' said mother

'Calm down Radhika, we cannot disrespect our son-in-law,' said dad.

Vinodji came searching for Sonali, once the crowd had paid their respect and left.

'Did you see how your sister behaved?' questioned mother.

'I did and I apologize on her behalf. I am grateful to Sonali for not creating a scene,' said Vinodji.

'Dignity of our family is more important than Karishma's childish behavior,' responded Sonali.

'Thank you Sonali, for always supporting me despite my family's ill behavior.'

I admired Sonali for her patience although, I disapproved of the idea of allowing someone to trample you the way Karishma did.

******

Venting out my anger on the wall, I smashed the ball hard on the wall and sprinted to keep up with it's pace.

'Hi,' said a familiar voice.

I turned around.

My eyes widened as I gasped at the sight of the man who had been my partner in crime.

'Oh god! Samar…What are you doing here?' I asked in surprise.

'Playing squash,' he responded cheekily.

Dressed in white shorts and an Under Armour tee Samar picked the ball and smashed it with the racket. I sprinted towards the ball, missing it as I hit my right shoulder against the wall.

'Are you okay?' asked Samar moving towards me.

'Yes, I am fine, let's continue,' I said.

It was my serve and Samar was quick to return the ball. Failing to strike once again, I excused myself.

'What's the matter Priya?'

'I cannot cope up with your serves. You are a professional.'

'That is not the reason Priya. It is lack of exercise.'

'Whatever the reason, I am exhausted,' I said.

'Then let's sit by the pool and chill.'

Samar plonked himself on the chair and ordered a glass of orange juice, while I ordered a chilli cheese toast and coke.

'Was your wife upset with you that night?' I asked.

'Fuming at husbands, is second nature to wives. If they didn't fume, then they wouldn't be wives,' laughed Samar.

Samar joked about wives, while I bit into my chilli cheese toast and sipped on my cola.

He finally excused himself to wash off the sweat with

a shower. A sudden downpour had me rushing out of the club too. I walked ahead holding my racket in my head with the hope of finding an auto rickshawto go back home.

Incessant honking had me turn around only to find Samar behind the wheel in a BMW. I hopped into the car thanking him. The fragrance of jasmine and air-conditioning on full blast had me sneezing.

'Are you cold?' asked Samar.

'No, it's just the fragrance, I am allergic,'

'I am sorry, it's the car freshener.'

A captivating beat played with sleazy lyrics.

'You like these *rasta chaap* songs?' I asked.

'I prefer old numbers,' he responded.

'Kishore ji is my favourite singer of all times,' said Samar as he inserted a usb into the usb slot.'

'Heard it before?' he asked.

'Yes. It may sound strange, but I am a fan of Kishore Kumar.'

He raised his hand for a high five.

'My wife hates it when I switch on old songs.'

'Your wife is ultra-modern.'

'We are opposites,' he said.

'Opposites attract. Don't they?'

'Attraction is short-lived,' said Samar.

The rains lashed harder on the wind-screen, the wipers moved faster and faster in synchrony.

The next song that played had us humming it together.

'You love soulful songs, like me.'

'We have a lot in common. We are both Bollywood buffs.'

Engrossed in the music we had passed my home and were heading towards Santacruz.

'Oh, we've passed my home,' I gushed.

'No problem, I can turn around.'

'Sorry, you must be late for work.'

'I work from home,' he said.

'What do you do?' I asked.

'I write lyrics for Hindi songs,' said Samar.

Stopping by a road side tea stall Samar ordered two cups of cutting chai and insisted I drink it. 'These are small joys in life. Rains, tea and songs.'

An hour passed by as we hummed songs and sipped on four cutting chais.

13

*"There is always some madness in love.
But there is also always some reason in madness"*
- Friedrich Nietzsche

With a bouquet of flowers in my hand, butterflies in my stomach and a heart filled with excitement, I stood at the arrivals gate of Mumbai Chatrapati Shivaji International airport.

'Stop behaving like a mule Priya, you are meeting him for dinner anyways, you don't need to go to the airport to surprise him,' Ritika had texted when I informed her of my plans.

Incapable of waiting till dinner time, I had impulsively left for the airport.

'Love has captivated your intelligence, you are delusional Priya,' Ritika responded.

Standing by the barrier, I watched the passengers exit the gate of the arrivals.

A skinny bearded chauffeur holding the placard with the name Ajai Mirchandani was chatting on his mobile, while the passengers walked past him.

Every person that I looked at was either holding on to their mobile or talking on it. Addiction to mobile could be considered as one of the vices of our times.

Checking myself on my phone camera, I dabbed a little colour to my lips as I held the bouquet of yellow roses under my armpit. The long wait was finally over as I watched Ajai walking out of the arrivals wearing a black leather jacket and denim jeans.

Breaking into a smile as he gazed at the crowd, his eyes searching for someone. Next moment, he slid his hand in his leather jacket pocket and answered a call. I guessed it was the chauffeur, as I anxiously waited to surprise Ajai.

Sliding his mobile back into his pocket Ajai walked in the opposite direction.

'Ajai,' I yelled, scuttling with my bouquet of flowers. My breasts dangling against gravity only to smash into a chubby saree clad woman. She abused me unabashedly while I stared at her crocodile bag. 'Don't you have any *akal*? Can't you see and walk,' screeched the middle aged woman.

My eyes following Ajai while the woman continued ranting.

'Your bag doesn't match your foul language. Instead of wasting money on a bag get yourself enrolled into a finishing school,' I retorted.

'You bitch,' screamed the woman as I scurried towards Ajai.

A sudden surge of emotion ripped through my stomach as I watched Sonakshi and Ajai enveloped in an embrace.

******

I had been running on the treadmill for the past ten minutes at the speed of eight. In those ten minutes my heart beat had risen and my legs felt weak. But I refused to get off, I had to be the master of my mind, not a slave.

Thirty minutes of running and weights had me exhausted mentally and physically. I limped towards the poolside and slumped into the chair.

'You look tired ma'am,' said the server, 'Should I get you a glass of juice?'

'Get me a cold can of coke please,' I said checking my mobile for messages. I messaged Ritika, 'Sonakshi was at the airport too. I felt like an idiot.'

'What did you expect Priya? She is his fiance`. Told you not to go. You were to meet him for lunch. What happened?'

'There is no message from him.'

'Please control your emotions before its too late.'

'What are you doing here?' asked Samar, 'I thought you were busy this morning,' wiping his face with his gym towel.

'I cancelled my plans,' I curtly responded as I wiped the mucus running down my nose, with my hands.

Samar pulled out a napkin from his gym bag and handed it to me. 'This is a napkin, one uses to wipe their mucous mucus, not their hands. Basic manners,' smiling faintly.

I blew onto the napkin and unintentionally handed it back to Samar.

'You can keep it,' said Samar, 'I have plenty clean ones at home,' he said. 'What's wrong Priya?'

'Nothing,' I wailed.

'You wouldn't be sitting by the pool and crying if there was nothing wrong,' said Samar as he stood up, 'I will meet you outside the club in ten minutes. We are going out for lunch.'

'I don't want to eat lunch,' I complained.

******

The eatery was small and the ceiling was carpeted with plants. We were seated by the wall of potted plants in the al fresco section.

The interior of the cafe was warm and at the counter were an array of cream cakes and pastries that caught my attention.

'Allow me to place the order Priya,' said Samar as the waiter approached us with the menu card.

Choosing a whole wheat bread sandwich for me and a banana, apple and walnuts smoothie for himself, Samar turned towards me.

'Let's hear about this man who has rocked your world.'

'How do you know that it was a man? It could be a woman?'

'Hmmm. Judging by your sexuality tendencies it must be a man. And if it was a catfight involving a woman you would have vented out even before I would have met you.'

In a few minutes that we had been seated, the empty café was bustling with people, occupying all tables.

'Self-importance,' I smirked.

'You can name it anything, I need to hear your story.'

'It's complicated,' I responded.

'I have always said, relationships are complicated.'

'Mine is confusing. I love a man who is engaged to be married. But he does not love me, the way I do.'

'Ae Dil hai Mushkil,' said Samar.

'What do you mean?'

'Have you watched the movie?'

I realized that Samar was talking about Karan Johar's movie.

'Your love is similar to the way Ayan had for Alizeh, one-sided.'

'Seriously. You are comparing my life to a movie?'

'Yes, what is portrayed on screen, is what happens

in real life too. Do you remember the scene where Shahrukh meets Ranbir?'

'Yes, I vaguely remember.'

'Despite being divorced Shahrukh loves his ex-wife.'

'What's the point Samar?'

'There is a dialogue between the two actors, *love is the most beautiful feeling in the world. There's nothing like the power of unrequited love. It's unlike other bonds that are shared. It's mine and mine only,*' said Samar.

'You are implying that I don't need Ajai to love Ajai.'

'Yes Priya, let me complete the lines. *If you gamble in the name of love, you must take it as there is nothing to fear. If you win, it's wonderful and even if you lose, all is not lost.*'

Holding my hands Samar continued, 'Never give up on love. Even if you lose, all is not lost'.

My phone vibrated.

'Maybe its him,' said Samar.

'It is,' I responded as I read the message.

'Hi Priya! I am so sorry for not communicating earlier. Have been busy shopping with Sonakshi. She surprised me this morning at the airport. I apologize but have to cancel our lunch plans. Will chat as soon as I am free.'

My phone vibrated again 'I hope to see you at the wedding.'

I did not respond.

'What is he saying?' asked Samar.

'Asking me to come for his wedding.'

'You must go,' said Samar.

'Why would I go for his wedding when he does not have time to meet me when he is here,' I grumbled.

'You are being egoistic. True love is devoid of pride and ego. You were talking to me about changing your habits Priya. This is the time for change. Control your anger, your hatred towards Sonakshi and accept the invitation with humility. Keep aside your pride,' Samar spoke with folded hands.

'Why are you pleading me to go? What difference would my presence make to Ajai,' I asked.

I resisted typing a confirmation.

'Priya, don't hurt him.'

'I will be there,' I typed.

'Your wife is a lucky woman. You are a good-hearted soul Samar.'

'If only my wife believed so. She wouldn't be with another man,' responded Samar.

I dropped my sandwich on the plate.

14

Samar's words, 'In the silence of love, you will get the spark of life,' a quote by Rumi were constant reminders to train myself to love Ajai unconditionally. Samar's revelation about his wife had me confused. How could Samar love his wife despite knowing that she was seeing another man?

Amrita had been cheating on Samar and believed that Samar had no idea. While Samar was aware of the on-goings, he continued showering her with love.

'To love someone else is her choice. To love her, is mine,' he said, adding, 'Envy and anger cannot be love. That is selfishness.'

The truth of Samar's life had me fumble as I sipped on the cappuccino. I read the Bhagavad Gita verses assimilating knowledge, but I lacked in wisdom. Wisdom only came when one's mind was pure.

******

Sonali had moved into a new home with Vinodji and her twins. Trying hard to adjust to her new lifestyle Sonali tried hard to hide her anger. Aashna and Aaryan were pulled out of their extra curricular activities. Mum's constant nagging on fighting for her right to inheritance made Sonali avoid visiting us.

'My friends avoid me,' cried Sonali when I visited her in her two bedroom apartment in Andheri.

'You will make new friends Sonali, right now you need to support your husband. Don't listen to mum.'

'Mum is not wrong Priya. Karishma has destroyed my home. It's not easy to let go off what we had. I think its unfair and my husband needs to realize that.'

'Give him time Sonali, I am sure he knows what he is doing.'

Leaving behind my family with their share of stress, I headed to the airport.

My folly of not booking myself online earlier had me seated in between two extremely oversized men. While one burped constantly, the other made loud wheezing sounds in his sleep. After takeoff, I requested the burping old man sitting on the aisle seat to kindly exchange seats as I was experiencing panic attacks sitting in the centre.

The safari suit man looked at me in dismay, 'Sorry madam, I have paid for this seat. Why will I give you?'

'I am sorry,' I responded, unable to fathom the fact that the airlines were out to extort passengers. The urge to use the washroom made me stand up after a few minutes requesting the portly man to move out. Not too happy to comply, the man took more than three minutes to stand up and step out of the little space. I walked towards the washrooms that were occupied.

Thoughts of Ajai bounced around in my mind as I waited outside the toilet. The last time I flew from London, Ajai had been on the same flight and I was not aware of this till he spoke to me. *Was it a coincidence that I dropped my passport or was I destined to meet him. If I was, then why was he marrying someone else.*

The descent had commenced, and I scurried back to my seat with a bladder I had finally managed to empty.

Once again the moustached man took his own sweet time to let me be seated. When he did stand up, he belched loudly on my face. The taste of sambhar had me woozy and the urge to smack him was rising within. The man did not even have the decency to apologize for his uncouth behaviour.

The flight descended at great speed dodging through the turbulent clouds and landing wobbly on the tarmac. I puked on the safari suited man, as I stepped out. His back covered with vomit.

A last look at myself in the mirror of the stinky washroom and wiping off the barf from my dress, I headed towards the luggage belt, feeling queasy.

Holding a placard with my name, I spotted a lean man dressed in an orange shirt and brown shorts wearing blue tinted goggles. Loser written all over his face.

'Myself Rakesh... Ajai's cousin from Jaipur,' spoke Rakesh after I introduced myself.

Kissing my hand, Rakesh welcomed me to the celebrations with a large grin that revealed his discoloured teeth showing tell- tale signs of being an addictive paan eater.

I wiped my hand with a wet wipe, on our way to the coach.

'That was a dreadful act!' I screamed as Rakesh spat out the red liquid on the pavement.

'Act? What act?' he asked.

'You just spat on the pavement. That is not done.'

'This is India...madam... you can spit. The rule of "No spitting" only applies in Singapore you know. I have family there and they say cannot spit, cannot even eat chewing gum. What *bakwaas* city, I say.'

'Not spitting on the streets, applies everywhere in the world,' I added with disgust.

'We pay high taxes to the government, let them do some work na.'

'Seriously...' I sighed and confirmed 'Are you Ajai's real cousin?'

'Any doubts madam,' Rakesh twirled his sunglasses just like Rajnikanth did in his movies.

'My name is Priya.'

'I know, I only bring the board sign.'

'*Do not let the behaviour of others, destroy your inner peace,*' read Samar's message as I tapped my mobile. I grinned as I read it. The message was apt for my agitated mind.

I messaged on my family chat on whats app of my safe arrival.

'Be on the lookout and don't drink too much,' was my mother's response

'She is Ajai's friend from Mumbai,' Rakesh announced to the old couple that sat in the front row looking frail and exhausted.

Murli and Mohini were Kamini's parents who had arrived from Jaipur, a few minutes ago.

I touched their feet as a mark of respect.

'May god bless you,' said uncle Murli pecking me on my forehead.

'You have good *sanskars* Priya,' said aunty Mohini kissing me on my cheek.

After a wait of ten minutes a young couple hopped on to the bus arriving from Mumbai but on a different flight. The couple moved past us without acknowledging our presence. I exchanged glances with Rakesh.

'They are from the girl's side. I know them. Sonakshi's cousin and her husband. No manners. Today's generation don't have courtesy,' whispered Rakesh.

My face puckered, as I too belonged to this generation.

'You are different. I can see. Very nice,' he added.

The driver was ready to go and Rakesh stood up to inform the few passengers that the ride would take half an hour and that we should avoid spitting from the bus all this while staring at me with a grin.

The strong scent of mustard oil and sweat was making me nauseous.

'Are you okay?' asked Rakesh, 'You don't look good.'

'Motion sickness,' I informed with the hope of his staying silent.

'You have loose motion?' he continued.

'No,' I answered, a little too quick.

'Here… drink water,' Rakesh handed me a bottle of water that he was holding onto.

Unable to resist my desire to puke, I actioned for the bus to stop and before Rakesh could give instructions to the driver, I had puked on his orange shirt.

Rakesh stood behind me massaging my back to help me ease the uneasiness. I felt uneasy with his back rub and moved away.

'You want to eat something?' Rakesh followed me as I hopped onto the bus.

Murli and Mohini expressed their concern, offering

me a mint sweet to chew on, when we hopped back into the bus.

Thanking them for their concern, I sat on my seat. Rakesh sat beside me, after wiping his shirt.

'I am sorry, I spoilt your lovely shirt.'

'Don't worry about my shirt, I have many like these,' said Rakesh.

The couple at the back seat continued their indifference to the guests from the boy's side.

After a twenty- minute drive and continuous banter by Rakesh, we arrived at the resort. Driving through the well pruned gardens, our bus stopped by the entrance of the hotel building and we welcomed to the loud sound of drums.

Kamini and Tina helped uncle Murli and aunty Mohini step down. Kamini embraced her parents and touched their feet as they blessed her and Tina.

Kamini's face turned pale the moment I stepped out of the bus. Greeting me with a cold 'Hello' she escorted her parents to the lobby. Rakesh held my hand as we danced to the beat of the loud drums

Rakesh introduced me to Ajai's sister; Tina as we swayed to the beats.

Ignoring Kamini, I thanked uncle Murli and aunty Mohini for their kindness and I headed towards my assigned room.

Escorting me to a spacious room, the bell boy placed my luggage on the luggage rack. Tipping him generously I shut the door of the room. I snuggled under the covers of the large bed and dozed off.

15

"There is no way to happiness. Happiness is the way"
- Thich Nhat Hanh

The camaraderie between the families was robust. Sounds of chatter and chuckle filled the dining hall. Rakesh had appeared at my door within half an hour of our arrival, ringing at my door bell incessantly. Dragging me to the breakfast hall, pleading I eat something before the pool party commenced. As we entered the large room that had a huge buffet laid for guests, my eyes spotted Ajai. Attired in a baby blue t-shirt, he was absorbed in conversation with a few white faces that stood out from the crowd.

I walked towards him, my eyes captivated by his charm. His face lit up as he saw me approach. Greeting me with a warm hug he whispered in my ear, 'Thank you so much for coming, I am so thrilled to see you Priya.' His melodious voice and gentle touch raising a storm within.

I jolted out of his embrace.

'Sorry, for not being present at your arrival. Sonakshi and I had a photo shoot early morning.'

'It's fine. I understand,' I responded.

'I hear you met my grandparents.'

'Yes. They are wonderful people.'

'They were praising you too,' said Ajai.

The statement made me joyous, as people rarely liked me.

'Infact, I knocked earlier at your door, but there was no response. I guessed you were resting.'

'I had dozed off,' cursing myself. *Damn*.

'Hope you are comfortable in the room?' asked Ajai.

Before I could respond. Rakesh interrupted, 'I am there bro, why you worry. I have taken good care of Priya Madam.'

'Yes, he has been taking good care of me besides entertaining me,' I giggled.

'Rakesh is a joker. Clean at heart,' Ajai rubbed his cousin's heart.

'Let me introduce you to my friends,' Ajai held my hand and introduced me to his friends.

'This is Pablo,' said Ajai.

'Hi,' said the blue-eyed hunk. Pablo scanned me as he shook my hand.

'This is Priya. My very good friend from Mumbai.'

I responded with a hello and pulled my hand away.

'Mike and Anne. Mike is my colleague Anne is Mike's fiance,' said Ajai.

'Hi,' I responded shaking hands with Mike and kissing Anne on her cheek.

Ajai then excused himself as Kamini called out for him.

Wearing a pink crochet top and white trousers, Sonakshi walked into the room with her friends. Welcoming all guests with an embrace and a huge grin with perfect teeth. Pablo acknowledged Sonakshi with a peck.

'You look beautiful,' commented Pablo.

Mike and Anne embraced her.

Rakesh introduced me to Ajai's fiancé.

'So, you are Priya Wadhwani, Ajai's close friend,' the sarcastic remark and her smirk were clues that she had heard of me.

'Yes, I am Priya Wadhwani. Ajai's good friend.'

'Glad to have you with us Priya. Hope you enjoy yourself at our wedding,' Sonakshi's voice trailed as she walked away to greet other guests.

'My room is not too far away,' said Pablo as he walked me to my room.

'Lovely, catch you later Pablo,' I shut the door before Pablo could push himself in.

I sat on the couch replaying Sonakshi's sarcasm in my mind. My mind was multi-organizing itself, placing toiletries, cosmetics, clothes, lingerie and at the same time thinking of Ajai and Sonakshi. My feelings were hopping from love and compassion to rejection and envy, did I want to organize my belongings or sort out my feelings for Ajai.

I dropped everything and sat on the terrace, lit a cigarette and checked my phone to distract my monkey mind.

A message from Ritika read, 'How does it feel attending your lover's wedding?'

'Missing you,' I responded.

'You can buzz me anytime. I am all ears,' she replied.

'No mum, there are no bachelors around,' was my response to mother's message asking me if there were any interesting guys.

Rakesh was too Sindhi besides being loud and I wasn't even sure if he was straight, while Pablo was Spanish.

I slipped into my emerald green swimming costume and checked myself out in the mirror. Playing squash had helped me tone my curvy body.

Tying my hair loosely into a bun, I slipped into a floral chiffon top and flip-flops.

'What the hell?' my words trailed, as I stood in shock when I opened the room door.

'What happened?' asked Rakesh. He was wearing a loud floral yellow and green shirt with printed floral red shorts.

'You scared me,' I screeched, 'I didn't expect to see you outside my door.'

'I am sorry, I was about to ring the bell when you opened the door,' said Rakesh.

'I must say you have great taste.'

'I know,' Rakesh beamed with pride.

'Sorry ha, I left you earlier in the breakfast room with those *goras*, but I had to see to a few works,' said Rakesh.

Rakesh's absence had gone unnoticed by me as I had been engaged in a long chat with Pablo.

'Priya, I just want to tell you something. You please keep away from these foreign peoples. Don't mingle with them. Last evening, they were taking drugs in the garden. They are not a good influence.'

'It's okay,' I responded, 'there is no harm in having a joint once in a while.'

Rakesh looked at me with dismay, 'You also take?'

'Not regularly. Sometimes at parties.'

Rakesh put his hand on his mouth, 'No. I cannot believe this. You are an Indian girl. How can you do that?'

'What has me being Indian got to do with me smoking weed and which century do you live in?' I sneered.

'I am from Jaipur. We live a very simple life.'

'I am from London and Mumbai. I have been a city girl all my life.'

The sound of loud Bollywood music echoed as we walked into the garden by the poolside. On the lawns were food trucks and each food truck had posters of Salman Khan smiling at us with his six packs.

'Why do you have Salman posters at a pool party?' I asked Rakesh.

'Sonakshi Bhabhi is a great fan.'

'Seriously?' I asked, 'I understand she is a fan, but posters on food trucks?'

'She loves Salman Khan and wanted to actually invite him for the wedding.'

'And?'

'Too expensive na,' said Rakesh creasing his nose.

'A wedding is union of two souls, not a concert for stars.'

Rakesh nodded in agreement as we picked up the green heart shaped goggles that were being gifted to the guests.

Few kids had jumped into the pool along with their fathers, while the women walked around in jazzy pool wear.

Waft of meat and fish filled the air whetting the appetites of the guests. My engagement to Gaurav had given me a glimpse of the efforts that went into organizing a wedding. Gaurav's family had designed a grand wedding. A wedding that would have been the talk of the town for months to come, if only it had materialised. I had learnt a lesson that an expensive and loud display of wealth at a wedding did not surmount to a good marriage.

While I ordered a vodka based cocktail for myself, Rakesh picked up a glass of orange juice for himself.

'I am a Hanuman bhakt.'

'Okay...so?'

'Saturdays, I pray to him.'

'Other days you don't?'

'Saturday is his day. I am extremely particular on that day.'

'So other days, he does not exist?' I teased.

Rakesh folded his hands, 'Don't discuss God like this?'

'Chill... I am pulling your leg... I totally understand.' 'You know Rakesh, when I was a kid, I also prayed to Lord Hanuman.'

'Really,' Rakesh's grinned, showcasing his stained red teeth.

'I read a small booklet given to me by my grandfather.'

'Hanuman chalisa,' responded Rakesh.

'Yes, I think it was that. It helped me sleep peacefully.'

'And now whom do you pray to?'

'Not any one God in particular,' I responded.

All idols from our home had been washed away in the sea, after grandfather passed away. My mother belonged to no religion, only a sect. We had no altar at home, only pictures of her Master.

'The couple has arrived,' the crowds muttered with joy. Pointing out to a buggy decorated with flowers. Watching the couple, Rakesh showered his *bhabhi* to be with praises. I ignored his comments and focused on Ajai.

Ajai had changed into a baby pink shirt and blue denim shorts and pink loafers. Stepping out of the buggy he held Sonakshi's hand, gliding towards the make shift dance floor. Sonakshi twinning with her fiancé, in a shocking pink long silk printed kaftan and a white floral band on her head.

'Seriously,' I muttered under my breath.

The couple then gyrated to the beats of Bom Diggy Diggy, while the crowd cheered loudly.

'What an entry!' exclaimed Rakesh.

I swigged the blue cocktail and helped myself to another one from the tray that the waiter was carrying around.

The couple was now mingling with the crowd and I followed their moves from the corner of my eye.

'How boring would weddings be if we did not have Bollywood numbers,' said Rakesh.

'Do you like Indian music?' he asked.

'Yes, but the soulful ones not these item numbers.'

I thought of Samar as Rakesh hummed a few numbers.

I quaffed on the pink cocktail and chose the green coloured cocktail as I watched Sonakshi nuzzling Ajai on the dance floor. Tina was dancing with Pablo, Mike and Anne in a circle. While Kamini, grooved with her friends. Everyone on the dance floor was bursting with energy.

'You should not be mixing drinks and too much alcohol will upset your stomach,' said Rakesh, as I guzzled on the green vodka based cocktail.

'Let's get you something to eat,' said Rakesh as he held my hand as I wobbled through the grass to the food truck.

I bit on the piping hot vada pav while Rakesh devoured a plate of pani puris.

Within the enclosed coffee shop sat uncle Murli and aunty Mohini with a few other old people. Uncle Murli was waving at us.

I tottered towards him and the next minute there was a loud bang.

Placing me on a chair as I sighed in pain, Rakesh pressed my head hard, the odour from his body making me nauseous.

'Are you okay Priya?' uncle Murli enquired.

Signalling Rakesh to bring some ice, the old man touched my head looking for bruises. Rakesh was back with ice, dabbing it on my head while I held my hand on my nose. Calming down after a while, I thanked them all.

'Nice to see you are fine. You scared me Priya,' said uncle Murli.

'I am sorry, I just miscalculated. I thought the glass door was open.'

'The important thing is that you are fine.'

'To happiness!' uncle Murli toasted.

'Rakesh is a very good boy,' said Murli sipping on his beer as Rakesh had volunteered to bring them street food from the trucks.

'Yes, very sweet,' I responded.

'Are you married?' asked one of the aunties sitting beside aunty Mohini.

'No,' I responded.

'You must be touching your thirties,' said the haggard woman.

'Not yet,' I curtly responded.

'Your parents must be so worried. It is very difficult to get a good boy once a girl crosses twenty five.'

'No, they are not worried at all,' I retorted seething in pain.

'Savitri, why are you asking personal questions,' Murli chided.

'In our times we had children by their age. Now-a-days girls want to enjoy life, drink and smoke but want no responsibility,' she continued.

Uncle Murli and aunty Mohini gave each other a fleeting look.

'It is their life,' said Mohini, 'let them decide what they want to do. And I think they are much happier than we were.'

'How can you say that, Mohini?' said the grumpy woman, whose white moustache was bushier than pubic hair, 'Children today lack values,' she added.

Rakesh was back with chaat from the food trucks.

'Savitri, why are you so pessimistic,' uncle Murli interrupted.

'How many marriages last today? Look at our Tina, she is divorced twice.'

'Savitri, it is her destiny It is no one's fault if the marriage did not work,' said aunty Mohini.

'It is the woman's fault if she cannot adjust,' Savitri responded.

'Marriage is a beautiful institution, if only there is an understanding between the partners. And if they don't get along isn't it better to move on in life, rather than stay and fight like you and Jaman did,' Murli jested.

Leaving sulking Savitri and the older generation debating on the younger generation, I plonked myself on a swan float in the pool. The pain had not been as miserable as the conversation the old people were having. To avoid Rakesh and his relatives, I floated away to the far end of the pool; away from roving eyes.

Basking in the sunlight and enjoying the silence, I had dozed off till someone held on to my feet, pulling me down into the cold water. Gasping for breath, I looked up. Sniggering, Pablo splashed the cold water at me, I too plopped my hands in the water. We giggled, as he then sprayed water at me with a plastic gun. I swam further away. Pablo followed me to the end of the pool. Drawing closer, he held me by my waist, his warm breath caressing my neck.

My body revelling with his touch, while my conscience gently tapped at my intelligence. My senses were engrossed in pleasure, but my mind was in a battle. The battle within continued arguing with itself, justifying. I was single; it was natural for my body to respond to its need. While my heart was in complete refusal mode.

My conscience bit me hard and I moved away from Pablo and lay on the sunbed.

My hat covered my face, sapped by the sweltering sun and the over doze of alcohol, I heard whispers of crowds chatting, water splashing and soft Bollywood music playing.

A mellow voice was calling out my name, but my lips were unable to respond.

'Hey Priya! Are you okay? What's the matter?' enquired a familiar voice. My mind tried to match the voice to the face but it failed.

Black out.

16

'The jealous are troublesome to others,
but a torment to themselves'
- William Penn

'How are you feeling now?' asked Rakesh as I gently opened my eyes, my head throbbing. Handing me a tablet and a glass of water, Rakesh drew open the curtains of the room.

Lying naked in a duvet, made me uneasy.

I tried jogging my memory as I popped a tablet handed by Rakesh, 'I am sorry, but I don't recollect anything. What happened?'

'I have no idea. Ajai called me to sit with you, so I came in here. He said you were sick and was worried for you. But he had to leave as the engagement party will begin in an hour. Infact I came in only a while ago.'

'Can you please leave Rakesh, so I can shower and change?'

'Are you sure you are okay Priya?'

'Yes, I am fine Rakesh. Thank you so much.'

'Okay, then I will come back in two hours to take you to the engagement. If you need anything call me on my mobile.'

******

Strapping my mother's heels and perfuming myself, I checked myself in the long mirror by the room door. I grabbed my clutch as the door bell rang.

Chewing on betel leaves, wearing a mauve blazer, paired with mauve trousers and a black shirt, hair gelled Rakesh stood outside.

'Nice hair style,' I complimented him.

'Thank you, I use mustard oil everyday,' he said blushing.

Who wears mauve trousers? I thought to myself. But corrected my thought. Without Rakesh around I would have felt lost at the wedding.

'Thank you Rakesh for being so kind. You have been extremely kind to me despite me being so rude to you,' I responded.

Rakesh eyes filled with tears as we walked silently towards the ballroom.

The entrance to the ballroom was lit up with shimmering candles in between metal grids lined with pink and white roses. As we entered I headed towards the bar.

Thoughts of Ajai were rumbling and tumbling

wondering if he had intentionally stepped in to change me. *Did he do anything?*

'You should not be drinking again,' said Rakesh, as I ordered myself a glass of martini.

'I am fine. Chill.'

My eyes explored the hall, while my mouth relished the apple martini. Kamini was chatting with her parents, Tina; dressed in a shimmery backless black gown, was in deep conversation with a middle- aged man. The newly married couple who had arrived at the hotel on the same bus with us were in midst of an argument.

I stepped outside for a smoke with a glass in my hand while Rakesh chatted with his families. In the corner of the lawn stood Pablo, Mike, Anne and a few others smoking. The waft familiar to my senses beckoned and I headed towards them. Handing me their joint, Pablo's intense eyes stared at me as I puffed on it.

Suddenly a hand pulled me away and chided, 'Why are you smoking weed with them? You're a good family girl, people will see you.'

'Don't you have anything to do Rakesh? Why are you tailing me?' I responded.

The kind words that I had spilled a while ago had once again transformed into rudeness.

'I have been instructed by Ajai to take good care of you,' said Rakesh.

'I am not a baby.'

'But I am doing what I am asked to do by the groom. You are a special guest. I also like you very much, Priya. You are a nice girl.'

'Thank you.'

'You remind me of my sister,' he added as his eyes trickled down a few tears. I was not sure why Rakesh was crying.

'My sister, Minal has been missing from the past two years and when I see you I feel I am with her.

'Missing? 'How old is she?'

'She was twenty when she went missing. It's been two years. One night, Minal was forced by her friends to attend the birthday party of their common friend. I dropped her at the banquet hall and left. I went back for her in two hours but her phone was switched off. So I entered the party and found most of the youngsters smoking *sheesha, taking drugs and drinking*. I hunted the place for her but she was nowhere to be found. I called her friends and they all said that she never came to the party.'

'And?'

'We never found her.'

'What? How can that be possible? Didn't the police help?'

'They have shut the case. They feel she has eloped with someone.'

Rakesh wailed as he slumped on the grass wailing, 'I miss my sister. I have no idea what happened that night. I miss her Priya, I miss Minal.'

I requested the waiter who was hovering around to get a glass of water. Sipping on water and taking a deep breath Rakesh continued.

'My mother has not spoken a word since then. She lives in a state of shock.'

The pain in Rakesh's eyes, made me feel guilty for treating him crudely. But that was not because he was Rakesh, it was because of me. It was my irritable nature that had me snap at people. I had tried hard to change in the past, but it was not easy.

A call from Kamini had Rakesh wipe off his tears and rush to the ballroom. 'Let's go Ajai and Sonakshi are walking in to the hall.'

Dressed in an ostrich feathered gown, colour coordinated with Ajai's velvet navy suit, Sonakshi looked stunningly beautiful as the entourage followed the couple playing drums and saxophone.

Breaking into a romantic number on the stage, Sonakshi mesmerized the crowds with her moves. After performing for the crowds Sonakshi seated herself beside her fiancé.

I bobbed myself on the bar stool, while Rakesh entertained the audiences. The pain hidden deep down, but his face was smiling with joy to see his cousin brother.

However tacky Rakesh was, his sense of humour had everyone in splits. Handing over the mike to a young couple called Manav and Pinky, Rakesh stepped down to perform with the family who were waiting in line.

Starting with young kids whose performance had the crowd clap gleefully, a parody had the whole family gyrating to Bollywood numbers, old and new. A feeling of remorse set in after watching everyone so joyous. *Are families so united as they seemed tonight? Why was my family different? Or was I different?*

Feeling light headed I stepped into the garden for a smoke. The fresh air helped calm my thoughts. Thoughts of how I always condemned my family, while Rakesh went out of his way for his family. Despite the throngs of pain he was experiencing he stood by his family in their happy moments. If only I could be like Rakesh, giving and loving. *Was it possible?*

'Hello again,' said Pablo.

'Hi.'

'I saw you come out from the hall. You don't like dance and music?'

'I do, but not so loud,' I responded.

'Then you like it soft,' he asked.

Pulling me towards the corner behind a tree, Pablo drew closer, pressing his lips against mine.

Pablo unzipped my gown while his tongue swirled around mine. I kissed back passionately, unbuttoning his shirt. In the midst, of my ecstatic moment, a hand pulled me away.

'What the hell are you doing Priya?' yelled Rakesh.

'What the hell are you doing here?' I yelled back.

'Zip yourself!' Rakesh ordered me, turning his face away.

I did so angrily.

Rakesh pulled Pablo by his unbuttoned shirt and slapped him. I pulled Rakesh away and slapped him back.

******

Pablo had left the scene while Rakesh and I sat in the garden, away from the crowd.

'I am sorry,' said Rakesh.

'I am sorry, I don't know what I was doing,' I responded feeling light headed and dizzy.

'I know I have no right to interfere, but I treat you as my younger sister, I want to remind you that men are animals, hungry for sex. Girls who allow men to take advantage have a bad name in society.'

This man was truly living in stone-age, I thought but I was too blank too respond. Kamini's call had us walk back to the ball room. As soon as we walked in Kamini ordered Rakesh to check on the service while Tina dragged me to the dance floor.

An hour of grooving had me sweat profusely and I rested on the bar stool. I watched Sonakshi dance with her friends. Dinner had been served and older people were walking back to their rooms after relishing their meals.

I gulped in a few more shots and walked towards the dance floor. Ajai's friends had him down a few shots while he tried to avoid it.

Throughout the party Kamini had watched my movements. When she walked out with her parents bidding good bye to Sonakshi and Ajai, I felt relieved. I went back on the dance floor. 'You dance well,' said Ajai joining me as he held me by my waist.

Imitating my steps Ajai danced along.

'Hope you are feeling better?' he asked.

'Was it you?'

Ajai's hazel eyes twinkled, he drew closer.

'Yes.'

Bringing himself closer, reeking of alcohol he bellowed, 'You are very beautiful Priya.'

My heart skipped a beat. *Was it the influence of weed or was it me imagining what I had heard?*

In a span of ten minutes, we were forced four shots into our mouth. I looked around unable to find Sonakshi.

'Where is your to be wife?' I slurred.

'Sonakshi has had too much to drink. Her parents

whisked her off to her room. She is under their supervision,' Ajai chuckled.

My heart jumped with joy and I danced like there was no tomorrow.

17

'Sex is the consolation you have when you can't have love'
- Gabriel Garcia Marquez

Ajai lay on my couch in a drunken state, one leg dangling down, and his tuxedo on the floor. 'Come here Priya….' Ajai slurred.

After I had entered my room an hour ago and changed into my pyjamas, Ajai had come knocking on my door in a drunken state.

'Open the door Priya,' Ajai had demanded.

My heart palpitated with ecstasy and apprehension on hearing to his voice.

'What are you doing here?' I whispered, looking around to check if anyone was loitering in the corridor.

Ajai rested his head on my lap as we seated ourselves on the couch. His sleepy eyes glowering with love.

Ajai gently hauled my face closer to his. With my neck feeling strained on the movement, I pulled away. Ajai pecked on my hand, caressing it.

'Your skin is so soft,' he murmured.

FINDING <del>MR. RIGHT</del> MYSELF

'Ajai why are you here?' I reprimanded.

'Aren't you pleased that I am sitting with you Priya, just you and me.'

'Tomorrow is your big day. Shouldn't you be resting. Beside, it's not right of you to be in my room so late at night,' I pleaded.

'Why not? You are my closest friend. Can't I spend time with you?'

'Not at this hour Ajai.'

'There are no time restrictions with friends.'

'Are we just friends Ajai? Isn't our friendship based on lies,' my body trembled as I spoke.

'What lies Priya?' mumbled Ajai as he sat up.

'Stop pretending Ajai, for god's sake, stop pretending that you don't love me,' I cried.

Ajai gently slid my hair behind my ears and wiped off the tears that trickled down my cheeks.

'You're so beautiful Priya,' his fingers caressing my face as he spoke.

'Is that all you have to say Ajai. I came here for you and you ask a cousin of yours to follow me around.'

'Priya what's the matter? Why are you so angry?'

I wept bitterly. I had no idea why I was behaving so stupidly. Why was I accusing Ajai, when I knew that he was getting married.

Ajai held my face pressing his lips on my temples.

'I am sorry if I have hurt you Priya. I know you love me, I knew it from the time we stood on those rocks as the rains moistened our bodies. From that very moment I knew I loved you too. But I had to comply to my duties. My duty towards my mother,' gently brushing his lips against mine.

Kissing me softly as he slid his tongue between my lips. The tidal wave of lust clouding my ability to think.

I resisted in a soft tone, 'Please don't.'

'I love you….' whispered Ajai.

A pleasant warmth suffusing my body, my mind debating of the consequences. A battle between the mind and my conscience was underway.

Ajai and my copulation had been a constant thought in my mind, since the past few months. That thought had manifested itself and how could I refuse this moment, I had much desired. How could I not get carried away with my emotions. My conscience too gave up the battle. The reading of the Bhagavad Gita, Master's guidance nothing mattered at this moment. Love won. Or was it lust?

******

At dawn Ajai had slipped out of my room. I lay in bed ruminating on the magical night that we had just spent together. There was a feeling of oneness that I had never experienced with anyone else.

Was it the alcohol or was it our love for each other. Morally we would be condemned for our action but technically, Ajai was not yet married.

Would Ajai stand up to his mother? Would he break off the wedding?

A thought of Pamela surfaced. *I had done to Sonakshi what Pamela had done to me.*

******

I was woken up by the incessant door bell. Smiling, I slipped on my robe and headed to open the door. In a red sherwani and beige churidar, Rakesh grinned at me displaying his paan stained teeth.

'It's 4:00 pm and you are still sleeping?' asked Rakesh, 'You didn't come for the *ghadi puja* this morning.'

'Sorry Rakesh,' I could hear my heart shattering. I was expecting to hear that Ajai had called of his wedding.

'Get ready fast, we have to join the *baraat*, they have already started dancing and all.'

'You go ahead, I will be there soon,' my voice was breaking as I spoke.

'What's the matter Priya? Are you crying?'

'Nothing....' I banged the door shut on Rakesh, before I let my feelings slip.

'I will wait for you,' yelled Rakesh 'even if I have to miss my brother's *baraat*, I will not leave you alone.'

Sliding my back on the door I slumped onto the floor and cried.

After half an hour, I emerged from my room, forced out by Rakesh's constant messages reminding me that he was waiting outside.

'You look beautiful,' said Rakesh as I finally stepped out in a plain lemon green *lucknowi kurta* and white *salwar* sans make-up.

'Has the *baraat* reached the bride?' I asked.

'Another ten minutes,' I think. 'Tina is very upset that I haven't joined the *baraat*.'

'I am sorry Rakesh to keep you waiting,' I asked, 'why didn't you go? My presence is of no importance.'

'It is to Ajai,'

I stared at Rakesh, 'Did he ask you to bring me?'

'Yes, and you must know that he tried to call off the wedding too. But aunty Kamini emotionally blackmailed him and he had no choice but to carry on with the wedding.'

I was happy and at the same time my heart cried in pain. Happy to hear that Ajai loved me but sad that we could never be together.

'All love stories don't have a happy ending,' said Rakesh.

By the time we reached for the procession, Ajai alighted from the horse, dressed in a gold *sherwani*. Welcoming us with fragrant garlands Sonaskhi's families offered us with sweets and cold beverages.

The rituals had commenced with Sonakshi's mother welcoming Ajai with *aarti* and applying *tilak* on his forehead. Breaking an earthen lamp with his heel, Ajai walked towards Sonakshi who stood behind a veil.

Ajai anchored his attention on me, as the priest tied the couple's hands with a pink *dupatta* that she wore around her neck. I looked away, my head spinning as reality was hitting hard.

The couple walked hand in hand towards the *mandap* that was decorated with red and white flowers. Standing tall in the green lawns against the backdrop of the beach, the four pilllars of the mandap signified the two sets of parents. Ajai's uncle represented Ajai's father for the wedding ceremony.

Reciting the Vedic mantras and lighting the holy pyre, the priest called upon all the gods and goddesses to witness and bless the two souls that were commencing their journey together for life. Hand in hand the couple circled around the fire promising to love and respect each other for life. The sacredness of the holy fire, the chants that reverberated on the loudspeaker aroused my conscience, my soul felt desolate and cheated. I strode out of the lawns, while the guests moved forward to congratulate the couple blocking Ajai forever from my sight.

18

*"The fire that warms us can also consume us;
it is not the fault of the fire"*
- Swami Vivekananda

After waiting for more than an hour in the sweltering heat, I registered myself and handed over my possessions at the counter- mobile, cigarettes and lighter. My eyes sheltered behind my Primark sun glasses; I headed towards the cottage assigned to me.

Ritika exhausted with my sullen behaviour had registered me into a meditation retreat.

'You need to gather yourself and know your true purpose in life. You are wasting your life behind a man, who chose duty over love.'

'Detach yourself from your emotions and you will set yourself free,' was Samar's advice when I had broken down at the squash court unable to bear the feeling of rejection and guilt. My family had been oblivious to my suffering. You have borderline depression said the counselor and a friend of Ritika's.

The door outside my cottage had three names Nadia Abbas, Geena D'souza and Priya Wadhwani. I peeped into the humid dark room and drew the curtains unveiling the views of a vast lush field.

'Hello, I am Nadia' A large woman in her fifties, dressed in a black long floral dress entered the room.

'I am from the Middle East.'

'I am Priya and I live in Mumbai. It's surprising that you have flown in to India for a meditation retreat,' I said curious to know why anyone would fly to stay in a retreat that provided no luxury. My own mother had persisted I go to a five star retreat. The idea of checking into a resort that asked you to bring the bare minimum, dress simply and share a room with two strangers appalled her.

'My husband just divorced me. One evening announcing talaq, talaq, talaq, I needed to get away,' said Nadia.

'I am sorry.'

'Don't be, I am glad he did. I am now finding myself instead of serving his needs,' Nadia walked towards the window. 'You mind if I take this bed by the window.'

Her words ringing in my ears, 'finding myself,' I responded 'please go ahead Nadia.' I picked up my quilt and hand trolley and dragged myself to the single bed by the door. No sooner had I placed my quilt on the bed and opened my trolley bag a young woman in her thirties walked into the room.

'Hello! I am Geena,' she grinned pulling a large suitcase. Nadia and I introduced ourselves to the husky voiced wide jawed woman. 'I have been assigned Bed A, so technically this is my bed,' she demanded.

'I am sorry,' I responded moving my belongings to the center bed.

'Where are you from Geena?'asked Nadia.

'I am from Poona,' responded Geena as she unpacked her suitcase. Out of which came pillows, bedsheets, quilt, towels, clothes, toiletries, medications.

While Nadia and Geena chatted amongst each other about husbands and children, I unpacked my trolley bag. *You have to learn to live with minimum possessions, you will have to wash your own clothes so take extra inners just in case they don't dry,'* Ritika had advised before I left for Igatpuri.

'And you Priya? What brought you here?' Nadia asked catching me off guard as my mind had wandered away once again to thoughts of Ajai. 'Depression,' I responded.

Their eyes filled with sympathy as they gazed at me. 'Oh Allah, what is with everyone being depressed. We have everything yet we are unhappy,' said Nadia.

'My depression is border line, it's not that bad.'

At that very moment a middle aged woman in a beige cotton saree walked into our room.

'Welcome ladies to our retreat. Please come to the main hall in ten minutes,' she announced and walked towards the window drawing the curtains shut. 'Please keep this shut. While you are in the room we don't want your attention to be diverted.'

'We need sunlight,' said Nadia.

'You will get enough when you step out, but while you are in the room we want you to be resting or meditating, we don't want your senses to be stimulated,' asserted the woman with her large brown eyes as she shut our room door.

'They want us to live in darkness?' asked Geena.

'May be that way we can see the light within,' giggled Nadia.

The briefing session lasted for an hour with volunteers assigning us our seats. Handing us our name badges, the volunteers reminded us of the signed agreement:

-no smoking during our stay,

-no physical contact with anyone,

-no meat,

-no killing

-and no talking.

It was a code of conduct that would have us sit in silence and not disturb the rest if we were unable to focus. I was avoiding any kind of eye contact with the rest of the women present. Wish I had read the documents before signing up. This was like a prison. Thankfully we were asked to move to the dining hall and grab a cup of tea before we took a vow of silence for the following ten days.

With tea we were served cookies. I sat in a corner overlooking the beautiful valley, hearing the chirping birds enjoying the soft touch of sunlight, 'You mind if I sit here?' asked Geena. I nodded, looking around for Nadia. Nadia had not come to the dining room.

'Where's Nadia?' I asked.

'She is with the volunteers asking questions regarding her diet. She requires proper meals and needs to eat to control her sugar levels. Guess they will give her special permission. She has brought lots of knick knacks along with her that they had kept aside,' responded Geena.

'Okay,' I responded.

'If she manages to get them back, we too can munch on her snacks when we are hungry,' said Geena, smiling.

After a short break, we took a vow of silence and thus commenced our ten day long meditation retreat. No form of communication was allowed except in case of emergency we could talk to the volunteer or respond to the teacher when asked questions.

Following the instructions of the soothing voice, we all focused on our breath and commenced our journey. Inhaling and exhaling gently, sensing the air that tickled the tiny nostril hairs inside. Focusing on my breath was a challenge and attaining peace of mind was the goal.

Unable to follow instructions to concentrate, I gently opened my eyes, to check what the others were doing. I looked around the dark room with fans whirling on the ceiling. There were around twenty women and on the side of the room were three volunteers, one of them was the middle-aged woman who had come earlier to our room. Another was a young girl, younger than me, she looked like she was in her teens and an older woman. All of them sat erect without any support. While the teacher dressed in a white salwar suit sat in front, her eyes shut. I looked behind for Nadia who was sitting on a chair and Geena on the left corner, her back supporting the wall. Why had I been assigned to sit in the front row that too in the center where there was no possibility of a back rest? Upset and irritated, I tip-toed out of the room heading straight to the washroom.

I sat below a tree on my return, gazing at the setting sun.

'Is everything okay?' asked a sweet voice. Behind me stood the young volunteer who was in a deep state of meditation a few minutes earlier.

'You can talk to me,' she said with a smile.

'Yes I am good, just find it difficult to do all this. I think I made a mistake,' I said.

'Being here is the biggest gift you can give yourself Priya,' said the young girl looking at my name badge.

'And you are?'

'I am Meera, I am a volunteer for this retreat,' she responded.

'You are young to be here, have you been doing this since long?'

'I started when I was twelve years old. And I can assure you that this was the best thing that ever happened to me. I top in my exams, I am grounded, happier and the best part is that I am aware every moment of my life.'

'Sounds good, but how can observing one's breath help to be happier?'

'Once you take the vow of silence and start the meditation you will reach a stage where you will feel activity in every little atom of your body. And you will see your past and your future.'

'I don't believe it,' I gasped.

'Our founder says that you don't have to believe in what he says you have to experience your own reality. And this reality is a reality only when you experience it yourself. But for that to happen you need to give yourself that chance.'

I tossed and turned all night, trying to throw off the bed bugs which crept up on me just like my thoughts. Unable to sleep, I sat up on my bed to practice what we had been taught this afternoon. I observed my breath. Observing whether it flowed from the right nostril or the left nostril. Just observing without controlling it.

I had not been able to control my feelings for Ajai, I had allowed myself to be carried away. But that moment was the most beautiful moment I had experienced and yet it had haunted me incessantly.

The teacher had lectured us on the mind last night, *'the behavior pattern of the mind is such that it doesn't want to live in the present. It rewinds and forwards itself and the moment you want to bring it to the present, it gets agitated.'*

Forcing my mind back to the present, I focused on my breath.

'When we generate any kind of negative thoughts in the mind, we manifest negativity into our lives. That is one of the laws of karma,' were my teacher's parting words.

I brought back my attention to the flow of my breath. In and out. In and out. In and out.....

Startled by a loud thud, I opened my eyes and looked around. Nadia lay on the floor. I hopped off the bed to help her as she chuckled. We were not allowed to touch anyone but this was an emergency.

'I am so sorry, I woke you all up,' said Nadia.

By then Geena too had woken up and was helping me lift Nadia off the floor, 'I am so used to sleeping on a king size bed,' Nadia snorted as she spoke and we all burst into giggles.

Standing in queue, below the night sky filled with stars and a waning moon, we waited for our turns at

3:45 am. Within fifteen minutes we had to report in the meditation hall.

We three walked through the narrow road towards the hall, being the last ones to enter. Nadia had taken forever in the washroom, while Geena and I waited in our track pants.

The process was the same, an hour of observation of breath. In, out, in, out,in, out. A loud snore from the back had us all wake up from our meditating sleep.

The teacher requested we focus on our breath instead of diverting our attention to those who had fallen asleep.

After a gruelling two hours of sitting in meditation, I and made my way limped to the dining room.

Munching on corn flakes and milk, I watched the birds flutter and play with their nestlings. No sounds, only the subtle crunching and munching noises filled the hall.

I ate three bowls of cornflakes, three bananas and gulped down two cups of tea. A quick shower in the tiny washroom and after washing my clothes, I headed back to the hall. My monkey mind was at it again. Random thoughts floated as my body struggled to sit still.

Meditating was far more tiring than any other sport or activity I had ever done. I had to step out of the hall after every fifteen minutes, either for fresh air or to use the washroom.

By the fourth day my mind had tamed itself to focusing on the breath, while my limbs continued being restless.

Five days had passed, and the teacher had incorporated another form of meditation. Sitting for two hours without moving was not for the weak. I packed my suitcase and headed to the quarters of the center head ready with what I had to say.

'I wish to leave,' I announced as tears streamed down.

My back, legs, arms everything ached. I had no way to communicate with my family. *What if anyone had fallen sick or died? How would I know?*

I missed my dad, my mum, my sister, my brother-in-law and my lovely twins. I needed to apologize to my family. I loved my family, they were the best and I missed them. I had never felt so much love for them. I needed to tell them that I was grateful to them.

The receptionist directed me to the teacher's room.

'Your family is doing fine. If there was any problem, they would inform us. I am sure they have our numbers,' the teacher smiled.

'What if they have lost the numbers?' I asked.

'We are listed, it will not be difficult. Priya you are worrying yourself unnecessarily. Four days have already passed, its a question of six days more. You are progressing well, how can you leave now?'

'My body is hurting.'

'It's not your body Priya, it's your mind that is resisting discipline and is sending signals to the body. Don't be a slave to your mind. Success only comes to those who complete what they begin. I am only asking you for six days of your life,' said the teacher with folded hands.'

'I am …on my way home,' I spoke on the mobile after we broke our vow of silence on the tenth day of the meditation retreat.' So glad to hear from you,' mum responded.

'I love you mum. I missed you, .. and…. Dad,' I choked and disconnected.

19

"Everything that is excellent will come when this sleeping soul is aroused to self- conscious activity"
- Swami Vivekananda

After I returned from my retreat that night dad had to be hospitalized as he suffered from dengue, his platelet count had fallen to around ten thousand and he was suffering from bouts of vomiting and nausea. From the time he was hospitalized mum spent her time in the hospital or the gurudwara praying for dad's recovery. We all breathed a sigh of relief after his platelets had started rising.

'I am glad to see you are better uncle,' said Ritika.

'It's all thanks to my wife, she has been tending to me with so much love,' said dad squeezing mum's hand.

'Babaji answered my prayers, I am so glad you are better now,' mum's eyes twinkled with joy.

'You take care uncle and I will see you at home now,' said Ritika as she stood up to leave.'I will drop her downstairs,' I said, picking up the visitor passes for Sonali and Vinodji to come up.

'We haven't had a chance to talk after your return from the retreat, how was the experience,' asked Ritika, as we stepped into the elevator.

'I have been meaning to call you but between the hospital and office I haven't been able to speak about it. It has taught me discipline and helped me calm myself. My thoughts are less random,' I said, stepping out of the elevator.

Greeting Sonali and Vinodji who stood away from each other, I handed the visitor passes to each of them and walked along with Ritika towards her car.

'Let's catch up and talk properly,' said Ritika as she stepped into her car.

Bidding her goodbye I walked back to the lobby of the hospital. Vinodji had gone up while Sonali waited down.

'Why didn't you go up?' I asked.

'You wanna grab a cup of coffee before we go up?' asked Sonali.

'What's the matter Sonali?' I asked as the barista handed us our cups of cappucino.

Spotting a table near the lift, we made ourselves comfortable in the chairs.

'I am planning to separate from Vinod,' said Sonali.

'Why?' I screamed. A few heads turned towards our direction.

'I am not happy with him.'

'But he is a good husband, why wouldn't you be happy with him?' I asked, 'Is this mum's idea?'

'I haven't mentioned anything to mum as yet. And I hope you don't. I have been in talks with a few lawyers,' Sonali wiped a tear from her eye.

'You love him, then why are you thinking of leaving him?'

Everyone's attitude has changed towards us since we have moved to a smaller house.'

'What has that got to do with you separating from Vinodji?' I asked

'We have no friends, no life.'

'But you have your husband and children.'

'I am frustrated Priya.'

'I don't want to live with a man who accepts things lying down,' Sonali argued.

'You two should visit a marriage counsellor, Sonali, you cannot give up on him at the time when he needs you the most.'

'He did not stand up for me when his family ill treated me,' said Sonali.

'It's not like they treated him well either,' I said.

'I cannot take this humiliation anymore Priya. He either

stands up and fights for his children's right or we leave him. Karishma needs to be punished for her evilness.'

'Let karma take its course. You need to surrender to the Universe.'

'Please don't talk to me about law of karma, Priya. It's all bullshit.'

'You are wasting your energy on Karishma. Instead focus on your children and your loving husband. Why don't you try meditating?' 'I have dedicated my life to my husband and children. And please don't start this nonsense of meditation with me,' retorted Sonali.

******

'This is the problem with our country. There is no professionalism!' Dad screamed on the phone still weak to get back to work. 'Dad relax I will handle it, I am looking into it,' I said attempting to calm him down. 'The production manager is sitting in front of me, we will find a solution,' I added.

'That idiot,' dad shouted over the phone, 'it was his job to have the samples ready for the shoot by last evening.'

'Prakash and I will make sure the photo shoot is not delayed, you don't stress yourself,' I disconnected the line.

All these days I had been attending to the administrative work at the office and never looked into the creative aspect.

'In three days, I will get the work done,' insisted the pot bellied manager.

I inspected the garments. 'These are practically completed, it requires only an hour of work, if few factory workers immediately sit down to compete it.'

'Yes but today is Friday, they will not come till after their namaaz.'

'Is there no other way?'

'We can give it to the job workers in Dharavi,' said Prakash.

'Then let's go and get it done,' I said, standing up with the samples in my hand.

'Madam, you cannot go there. It's very dirty,' said the grumpy manager.

'Since you don't go, I will have to Prakash.'

'Madam, our workers can do it when they come, I will push them to complete by tomorrow.'

'It should have been done by yesterday. We are heading for Dharavi to get this work completed. And the expense that the company will bear for your laziness will be deducted from your salary, Mr Prakash,' I said handing him the samples. 'Now let's carry those and get the job done,' I demanded.

I was in no mood to accept a no or allow the work or the company to be treated as a joke. Planning and executing was vital in any business and Prakash had been unable to execute the plans that my father made. Yet my dad let him continue as manager.

'Prakash is a good person, but I need to be hovering on his head,' my dad would often say.

'If I needed to be attentive of my manager, why would I have a manager,' I had asked.

'Priya you must understand, Prakash has been with us through thick and thin.'

'You have been through thick and thin. This man is just tagging along.'

With Rajan in tow, we headed to the factory that was located in Dharavi area which is considered one of the largest slums in Asia. The narrow streets were laden with rubbish and filth. Covering my nose with my scarf, we climbed up the tiny stairs to the small make shift factory of skilled job workers who sat crouched in a small room working on garments. Paying them a large sum of money to place on hold the work they were doing. Prakash handed over the samples, instructing them on the requirement of each garment.

Whilst the workers began working on our garments, I stepped out of the stench filled room and stood outside on the narrow street watching the passers by. The area was one of the most crowded places I had ever been to in Mumbai. Prakash stepped out of the room too.

'How do these people stay here?' I asked Prakash.

'The deprived have no choice Madam, all they want

is a roof on top of their heads and two meals, these job workers work day and night. At times without even taking a bath,' said Prakash 'life is not easy for the under priveleged.'

'Where do you live?' I asked.

'Not too far away from here Madam.'

'How many of you?'

'We are six of us living in a tiny room, my old parents, my wife and two children.'

I felt guilty for threatening Prakash with a salary cut.

'I am not lazy Madam, at times I am just broken and frustrated,' said Prakash.

Life was not easy for anyone. Everyone is dealing with their own issues and judging them was unfair. I promised myself to be careful before accusing and judging. Prakash had his flaws but all humans do.

With the samples in tow, I headed to the shoot. Handing over the samples to the team I headed back to the office while Prakash supervised the shoot.

Dad had been very pleased that I had accomplished what I had promised. But for me it was not about the accomplishment but the lesson that I had learned for the day. I had judged Prakash when in reality I had not known the reason for his slackness. The lesson of being sympathetic and empathetic towards those who were not as privileged as I was.

20

'The wound is the place where the Light enters you.'
- Rumi

'Are you still brooding over him?' asked Samar as he smashed the black rubber into the wall so hard that it bounced on the glass.

'I am trying not to think about him.'

Samar missed the ball as I served.

'You are avoiding your feelings, then. Feelings don't die however deep you bury them. You have to know how to live with them in peace.'

'My feelings are dead and burnt, not buried.' I won the game point.

Having cappuccino after our set of three games had become a ritual, every Sunday. Separated from his wife, Samar spent his Sunday mornings at the club.

'I am moving to Delhi for good,' he announced.

I placed the cup back on the table.

'Why Samar?'

'I will join my dad's business,' said Samar.

'And your dreams of writing and producing a movie?'

'Hopefully, I will do so when I am in my sixties.'

'Besides Ritika, you are my only friend in Mumbai,' I scowled.

'My dad has been diagnosed with cancer Priya. Right now his health is a priority not my dreams,' said Samar.

Despite the pain that Samar had gone through in the last few months, he had been sturdy. While his wife spent time with her lover at the club, Samar spent his days travelling in hope of his wife's return.

'And Amrita.' I asked.

'She will come back to me. I have faith,' said Samar.

His optimism at times made me believe that he was delusional I was being judgmental, I reminded myself.

'All the best Samar, I hope your true love wins.'

******

In our living room, sat a young man chatting with my parents, along with a skinny middle-aged woman.

Mum sauntered towards the passage.

'Priya hurry up and come to the living room. Please apply some rouge and lipstick.' I took my own sweet time and freshened up and entered the living room dressed in a comfortable long printed skirt and white top. My mother looked at me with disapproval.

'This is Priya. Our daughter.'

'And Priya this is Ravi Tilani and his aunty Nitya. Ravi is from Singapore. Nitya lives in Mumbai. She is a very good friend,' said mother. *One more friend to my mother's long list of good friends.*

I greeted the stubby round faced man as we shook hands.

'Priya get the dinner laid on the table *beta*.'

I had no idea why my mother insisted on me going to the kitchen when her staff was well trained to serve dinner.

'Madam wants to create a good impression on the guests,' said Supriya when I entered the kitchen.

'Yes in the end all marriages are about men subjugating their woman,' I tittered.

Our guests were pure vegetarian and Ramu had prepared an amazing feast for them, *chole bhature, sai bhaji, pulao, peas paneer, roti and raita.*

Mum served Ravi with zest feeding him as if there was no tomorrow.

'Enough aunty my stomach will burst, if I eat one more bite,' said Ravi.

'You know Ravi does *seva* at the *satsang ghar* in Singapore,' said mum.

'What kind of *seva*?' I asked.

'I serve water at the *satsang ghar,*' said Ravi with a faint smile.

'That's amazing,' I jested 'serving water at the *satsang ghar.*'

'And what do you do for a living?' I asked.

'I am into investing in real estate,' said Ravi.

After the meals were over Ravi and dad discussed the share markets, while mum and Nitya discussed me.

'Priya meditates everyday without fail. She did this retreat and it really changed her for good,' said mum.

'That is why she looks so calm,' said Nitya.

The discussion had me as the topic without me being a part of it.

'I love you Priya.' said mum as the guests left. 'I hope this works out. Ravi seems to be a very good guy.'

'He is ok,' I responded.

'I pray to Babaji that Ravi says yes.'

******

Next morning my mother had waited impatiently for Nitya to call. And when she did, mother and Nitya arranged for a dinner date.

At sharp 8:00 pm, Ravi picked me up from home.

Scanning through the menu, I chose the roasted chicken with mashed potatoes while, Ravi ordered for himself a penne arrabiata and grilled vegetables.

'Your mother is a follower of Babaji, and who do you follow?' asked Ravi.

'I am not a follower of any sect, I believe in the power of the Universe.'

Not interested in conversing about Babaji, I steered the conversation towards Ravi and his past but all that I could find out was that his parents had passed away a few years ago in a car accident. He did not speak of any woman in his life. While I shared my story about Gaurav and made sure, I did not mention Ajai.

Ordering a bottle of rose wine Ravi spoke of avoiding eating non-vegetarian.

'Besides the fact that one cannot meditate for four hours after eating non-vegetarian and also did you know that chicken is the most genetically manipulated amongst all animals? They are forced to grow sixty-five times faster than their bodies normally would.'

I bobbed my head side ways as I had never taken any interest in knowing how it came to my plate to begin with.

'You know chickens are housed in giant overcrowded sheds and packed in by thousands. They are forced to stand and sit on filthy manure laden flooring.'

I gulped the wine. I had toyed on the idea of

becoming a vegetarian after the retreat, but that episode had lasted for two weeks.

Moving the little vase of blue harvest bells and the candle stand, the waiter placed a silver bowl of varieties of hot bread on our round table. I picked the white cut loaf and buttered it while Ravi took the multigrain bread and nibbled on it.

The maître served our meals. The roasted chicken with mashed potatoes was glazed with butter with a few veggies on the side in an oval white gold lined plate. I pierced the chicken with my fork and slit it open, letting the juices flow.

'I must tell you this Priya, the other day I read this article in which they spoke of chicken litter.'

I wanted to pierce his eyes with my fork. Hypocrite.

'It talked about how, chicken litter containing arsenic is fed to cows in factory beef operations. The arsenic that's pooped out by the chickens gets consumed and concentrated in the tissues of cows, which is then ground into hamburger.'

I placed my knife and fork back on my plate and glared at Ravi, as he bit on a large piece of bread soaked in his vegetable juice.

'I understand that eating animals is religiously wrong and honestly I am working on it but not because someone has asked me to forgo it. You're a vegetarian not because you love animals, but because your Babaji has asked of you to be so.'

'Isn't that important. I mean your mother follows Babaji too and she too does whatsoever our Master preaches and guides us to do,' responded Ravi.

'That's what I am trying to say that you are doing it out of love for your Babaji not for the love of animals. There is a difference.'

'I don't understand. What is the difference?' Ravi shrugged his shoulders as he spoke, 'Priya our path teaches us to be sympathetic and empathetic towards all beings unlike other paths. Our Babaji teaches us discipline and service.'

'I am sure he does. I have nothing against him, as I respect all the Masters who work towards the rise of humanity. But may I ask, how is it that you don't consume meat but the strap of your watch is made of animal skin and those loafers you are wearing, aren't they made of calf skin?'

'Never thought of it this way. But I guess, till you are not eating it, its fine,' said Ravi, flatly.

21

"Wherever a man may happen to turn, whatever a man may undertake, he will always end up by returning to the path which nature has marked out for him."
- Johann Wolfgang von Goethe

'Diet Preferences cannot be a criteria for not liking a boy,' argued my family. Ravi is a good boy. You will be happy with him,' reiterated mum.

'I don't need a man to complete me,' I responded, 'Mum, I am happy staying single,' I pleaded as we sat in our living room.

'Listen to your mother, she is right. Ravi is a good boy Priya,' dad added as he looked up from his newspaper.

'You have no reason not to like Ravi. He is good looking,' Sonali tittered.

'What is with you all? Don't you all get it? I feel nothing for him. There has to be some kind of chemistry...I don't feel anything,' I complained to deaf ears.

Dad did not look up and mum stepped out to instruct the staff to serve lunch, while Sonali played with her twins.

I went to my room once Sonali bid adieu. Mum and dad were not too pleased with the fact that Sonali was spending more time at our home than hers. Although Aaryan and Aashna's presence brought joy to their life, they would have liked their daughter to spent more time with her husband. Nothing was going right for our family. Dad's business was going downhill, so was his health and he constantly complained about joint pains and a weak stomach. Mum was guilty of interfering and brainwashing Sonali against Vinodji. If only mum would have not sparked the fire that had ignited after Chandra's death.

Mum was thrilled when Nitya had called to confirm with a yes from the boy's side. Ravi was ready to marry me and Nitya had discussed the wedding dates with my parents. Mum was obsessed with my marriage and had registered me with online dating sites without my knowledge. I was livid when I found out and blasted her that evening when Ritika had called to inform me that she had seen my pictures on a dating site.

'I was browsing dating sites, along with my young nephew and came across your name.'

I had barged into my mother's room and accused her, abused her and walked out in a huff.

I tossed and turned all night in bed. I even tried to meditate but failed. Half way through the night I had an epiphany, *I was not angry at my mother, I was angry with myself for not being able to find someone who loved me truly.*

Would I find someone? Was I disillusioned with life? Why was I still attached to memories of Ajai?

A knock on my room door brought me back to the present moment. Dad peeped into my room, 'Are you free to talk?' asked dad.

'Yes,please come in,' sitting up as dad plopped himself on my mesh chair, by the desk. 'I am sorry,' said dad.

'Please don't say sorry, I should be sorry.'

Dad stood up from the chair and sat beside me on the bed. His eyes glancing at the Bhagavad Gita placed on top of the night table. Picking it up he touched it on his forehead, 'Grandfather gifted you this sacred book on your eighteenth birthday.'

'Yes, he did.'

'He loved you girls more than he ever loved me,' said dad.

Dad was right, grandfather loved us and spent more time than dad ever had. When I was teased for the color of my skin or humiliated for being overweight, I ran to my grandfather. He would tell us stories of his time in Pakistan and made it a point to attend our annual days.

'I missed out on your growing years and have never been there when you needed me. I want to tell you that, I love you Priya and thank you for being you.'

******

Next morning I headed to the *durbar* to visit the Master and seek his blessings. Master had not returned from Haridwar. I was looking for an answer but was unable to find one. I called Ritika for advise, who suggested to follow my heart. There was a feeling of guilt surfacing within. Guilt of not obliging my parents with their wish.

I sat in the sanctum staring at the gods and goddesses hoping that they would guide me in some way, waiting but there was no definite answer. My heart and mind were playing truant. A yes to please my parents, a no to Ravi's bookish jabbering, a yes to the fact that he loved me, a no for the fact that I did not love him. The inner conflict grew. I pulled out a paper from my diary and tore it into two. I scribbled a Yes on one and a No on the other and folded them. Tossing them in between my palms, I the placed it below the altar. I shut my eyes, folded my hands and prayed for guidance. I picked up one chit and glanced at it for a while. Dumping both chits in the bin, I headed home.

With a huge bouquet of roses in his hand and wearing a navy blue silk churidar kurta, Ravi walked into our house along with Nitya and her docile husband Vashi. A houseboy and chauffeur waited outside holding on to a huge basket and two trays. Ramu and Supriya collected the gifts and placed them on the coffee table in the living room. Mum scrambled to save her much adored Swarovski duck from the center of the table, 'What is all this Nitya? You are from the boy's side, you don't need to bring so much.'

'Let's not start this boy girl side nonsense. Priya is my daughter too and this is for her,' said Nitya picking up one of the trays, placing it on my lap and kissing my forehead.

Vashi and dad were busy chatting when Nitya called out to her husband, 'Listen dear, you can talk later first lets complete the engagement ceremony. C'mon Kamal it's your daughter's engagement let's get it going.'

'Sonali please get the ring from the cupboard,' mum chimed.

'You look beautiful in a saree,' whispered Ravi his twinkling eyes scanning me. I played with the edges of the digital lime green saree.

Sonali returned with a red floral shaped velvet box. The rings were placed on the trays along with red petals. Ravi slid a three carat diamond ring set in white gold onto my finger and I slid the ring that had been made for Gaurav.

******

Next morning we headed to mum's good friend, Chahna's son Ameesh Chopra's store to find a wedding lahenga for me.

Once again, I was bestowed with roses and I was upset.

I needed to tell Ravi that I disliked to see blooming flowers die after a few days in my living room.

Ameesh Chopra sat in his massive office. Sloe-eyed and high cheek boned, like a Greek God. My mother's eyes surveying him as we sat down. Everyone knew that Ameesh was dating a famous filmstar, though they both denied it to the media.

'Congratulations Priya!' said Ameesh extending a warm hug. I responded with a thank you. He asked us to follow him to the store instructing the sales girl to show us his best creations. Each outfit was not less than three lakh rupees and weighed a ton. I found myself suffocating in its weight and the high cost.

'This one looks so good on you Priya,' said mother walking into the trial room. 'I can't seem to zip it. It's too tight for me.'

The attendant informed us that was the biggest size available.

'Are all brides so thin?' I asked the pretty attendant.

'No, there are many healthy ones too. We can customize it to your size.'

'Thank you,' I said sarcastically, 'you can wait outside now. Mum can help me undress.'

She fake smiled.

'Mum it's ridiculously over priced,' I whispered as soon as the attendant stepped out.

FINDING ~~MR. RIGHT~~ MYSELF

'That's the standard price, we will get a discount.'

'We are having a simple temple wedding, why should we spend so much?'

'Because it will be all over social media. And Ameesh Chopra is one of the most coveted designers,' whispered mum as we walked out of the changing room.

'So did you like the *lahenga*?' Ameesh's husky voice echoed in the store.

'It's very pretty, a little tight though,' I responded, 'although I would prefer wearing a saree like mum did at her wedding.'

'The red sequence saree,' laughed mum 'that's outdated.'

'Sequence is in fashion aunty, I have a huge collection of sequence sarees too.'

The pretty attendant walked with us to the rack. After draping five of them, I asked if he could make something like my mum had worn. He asked for a picture. Swiping through the gallery, I enlarged mum's wedding picture.

'It's so pretty, oh my god, so classic and elegant and aunty you look ravishing,' Ameesh had nailed it, praising mother meant she would not create obstacles in my decision to wear her saree. I smiled inwardly.

'You think I could wear this one,' I did not want my parents to overspend on a saree that I would never wear again.

'Actually we could work on it and I can assure you it will look brand new. Do you still have it intact?' asked Ameesh.

'Yes, I am very particular about storing my belongings.'

Within an hour we were back at Ameesh's store with mum's red sequenced saree.

******

The priest commenced the rituals as I sat with with my head tilted, touching Ravi's head. The over zealous English speaking priest briefed the crowd about marriage. 'What is Marriage? he asked and answered himself, 'a marriage is not only a union of two people, it is union of two souls whose karmas have been attached. The god of fire, Agni devta is the witness to this holy union. When two souls unite the gods and goddesses shower them with blessings as they pledge to fulfill their vows of duty *(dharma)*, of mutual financial arrangement *(artha)* and intimacy *(kama)*.'

I was announced Mrs. Malvika Tilani as Ravi slid the *mangalsutra* around my neck and *sindoor* on my forehead.

'From today onwards you are first Malvika Tilani, wife of Ravi and then our daughter. Leave the old Priya behind and start a new life, a new beginning. Our blessings are with you,' were dad's parting words as we bid goodbye at the terminal.

******

In between silent snuffles, I sipped on the tawny port wine while Ravi slept immediately after takeoff. Red and gold bangles jingled loudly as I swigged the wine.

22

'Chains do not hold a marriage together. It is thread, hundreds of tiny threads which sew people together through the years.' - Simone Signoret

One year later

Shutting off the alarm that read 2:59 am, I sat up on my bed watching the tip of the prideful mountain that swathed in silvery light. Stars twinkled in the sombre sky, while the valley sat in tranquillity.

Waking up dispirited, with my eyes half open I focused on the red light above my drawer. The three shelved wooden cabinet posited my three white sarees with blouses, a Himalayan face cream and a comb. On the night stand, beside my single bed, stood the Bhagavad Gita.

I rubbed my eyes trying hard to shake away the deep slumber that continued forcing itself, enticing me into the sweet world of dreams. Finally jerking myself away from its alluring embrace, I headed to the tiny washroom attached to my single dormitory. The toothpaste that I had abhorred had now become my preferred brand. Buy Indian, wear Indian, use Indian had become my motto.

Dragging my sleepy self towards the tap that streamed ice cold water I filled the plastic bucket and bathed with the help of a mug. The cold shower shook my body, expunging away the drowsiness that had slithered in.

I dragged myself to the small meditation room that was diagonally opposite to my allocated room in the dilapidated four floored building. During the day, the sights of the mountains from the corridors were breathtaking but at 3:30 in the morning, the darkness and the silence were eerie. Opening the aluminium framed netted door I walked into the tiny room. A few sisters sat in the room gazing at the picture of their Master with reverence. I stared at the bright light breaking into a few yawns.

Ravi is a good boy, he is your husband. You need to change yourself. You want to bring shame to our family also, your sister is troubling us enough and now you too. You girls want us to die soon. Mum's words replayed in my mind.

I felt a sharp pain ripping through my stomach. I winced as I stared at the bright light for a while but the waves of thoughts circled and the circle grew wider. The wider the circle grew, the awareness of my pain intensified.

I bowed and walked out of the room, holding on to the end of my saree. I scurried to my room, shut the door and vaulted into my single bed.

******

I stayed up till late till Ravi came home from work. He spent Sundays at his spiritual center, Friday nights with his boy gang, Monday nights with his business associates. During the remaining nights he was too tired to go out. The few times that he was home, we ended up in an argument and landed up sleeping in different rooms. Ravi didn't let me work, he wanted me to go out and socialize. But social outings did not satisfy me. At times I joined Ravi at his spiritual center to please him. But I failed at that too.

I woke up with a splitting headache and a growling stomach. Rays from the sun were streaming in through the white translucent curtains, gently caressing my face. I sat up, staring at the picture of the Master on the wall of my room. The ashram belonged to him, he was no more yet he lived in the hearts of his devotees.

Where we resided there was no kitchen and our only source of food was the canteen that was across the road within the ashram campus. Besides a large canteen, the campus boasted of a large auditorium, a museum, a meditation hall, a state of the art building for more than five hundred guests and cottages for the seniors who had served the ashram for the past fifty years. The devotee brothers were incharge of serving the meals that were prepared by the sister devotees. Menus were fixed for the month. Today was Thursday and today's breakfast was *poha* and a banana. The brother devotee greeted me, '*Om Baba*' with a toothless smile as he served *poha* onto my stainless steel *thali*. Pouring myself a glass of milky tea, I walked to the far corner of the canteen avoiding any eye contact with other brothers and sisters.

For breakfast, lunch and dinner I sat on the same chair

beside the window. My eyes were fixed at the main gate as I chewed on the oil soaked poha. The breakfast was always the day's worst meal. I peeled the banana and slowly took a bite watching the devotees brothers and sisters strolling in and out. Some common men came into the campus to attend the lectures that were held every morning in the meditation hall.

A large number of guests were off loading from the buses that stood outside the gate.

For the next few days these guests would be living in the campus and attending the many lectures. One of the lecturers in the event would be Sudha, she had returned last night from a world tour. Sudha, was one of the most revered sister. The first time I met her was in Singapore when she had come for a three day retreat. I had found a friend, guide and a big sister in Sudha during those three days.

I picked up my plate, spoon and glass and washed it in the basin. Wiping them dry, I placed them back on the rack. I walked to the main office at the entrance of the campus. I had to finish my pending work, to attend to Sudha's talk. I sat on my table and sorted out the many letters that the organization received. The one's that were worth reading went into a blue file that I would hand over to the Head and the unworthy ones's went into the bin.

One thousand eager listeners waited for the woman sitting on the dias to start speaking. Sudha sat with her eyes half open, on the white satin upholstered sofa. In front of her was a wooden coffee table and a microphone placed on a stand. The hall shone in the dim red light.

Sudha gently opened her warm compassionate eyes that scanned the crowd with a radiant smile. 'Om Baba,' she said softly and the crowd responded back. Sudha was a celebrity, her talks had influenced many a lives and people all over the world adored this petite, soft spoken woman.

Sudha began her lecture with questions. Questions that involved self reflection. Today her questions were based on relationships, as the title of her lecture was 'The importance of Relationships'.

'How many of you feel relationships are complicated?' Many hands were raised in the crowd. Mine stayed on the sides of the chair. 'How many of you feel betrayed by your relationships?' Once again many hands went up. 'What is the reason?' asked Sudha. Voices echoed in the large hall. 'High expectations, lack of patience, ego, misunderstanding...'

Sudha smiled and asked the crowd to keep themselves in mind and introspect, 'Don't think of others, think as you. Do you have high expectations, are you patient, is your ego massive. Everyone feels that they do a lot for the other person but get nothing in return. We are hurt not because of them, we are hurt because we keep expectations from them.'

******

I struggled to keep my eyes open. Covering my face with my saree, as I yawned.

******

The dinner party with Ravi's business associates and their fancy wives were unappealing to me, but I tagged along. I was working on my marriage and complying with my duty as my parents had asked me to do. But throughout the party, Ravi was socializing without me. A woman by his side, I recognized her from her pictures on facebook.

The music was getting on my nerves and I requested Ravi that we leave. Unobliging to my wish, Ravi instead suggested that I leave with Deepak, his partner and father to a new born baby.

With the excuse of finding a gas station Deepak deviated from the path to our home and halted the car in a quiet street.

When I questioned Deepak, he locked the car doors and slid his hand through my chiffon saree. Thrusting himself on me, he grabbed me by my hands and tied them with his tie.

'Please leave me,' I howled as I pulled the lever to open the car door.

Smacking me hard and lowering the seat, Deepak unleashed the animal within him.

******

I woke up to a loud thunderous applause that reverberated in the hall. Sudha stood up with folded hands and walked down the dias. With a gentle smile, Sudha greeted me in the hallway.

'How are you Priya?' asked Sudha as we walked towards the garden.

'I am fine,' I responded.

'What have you decided?'

'I am confused. I want to live this life but at times I feel guilty, as I miss the little comforts that I was used to. And beside the food here is lousy.'

Sudha smiled in agreement, 'Yes it is.'

'You are still attached to the materialistic world Priya. Life of a monk is not for everyone. It requires a lot of will power and love for God.'

'I love God.'

'God resides in each of us Priya,' Sudha's secretary brought in a message as we sat on the bench in the garden.

'Ask them to wait. I will bring her,' Sudha instructed her secretary.

'Living a balanced life, performing one's duties and spreading love are a few ways of expressing love to God. One does not need to run away from the world to love God. I let you experiment the kind of life monks live. Now, it's time to go back to the world and spread the message of love.'

I looked at Sudha with tearful eyes.

'They are waiting to take you back, Priya.'

23

"A great relationship does not happen because of the love you had in the beginning, but how well you continue building love until the end." - Anonymous

The drive to the airport was tranquil. No conversations, only an air of mourning. My parents were mourning their daughter's bad karmas. A life of abstinence was not something parents were comfortable with for their children.

'Be conscious of your every act in the world. What you give, you get back ten-fold. Give love and compassion and you will receive the same. You don't need to meditate daily but be meditative in your actions. Living a life of a monk is far easier than living in the world and away from it. This is your challenge Priya,' Sudha's parting words were ingrained in my mind.

Like my life, the flight back to Mumbai had its turbulent moments and there were passengers who were undisturbed and enjoyed the journey, while some held on tightly to the armrests of their seats.

Each one of us makes the choices that define our journey.

A frail Sonali waited at the exit of the terminal with her twins. Aaryan and Aashna embraced their grand parents but hid behind their mum when I drew closer.

'They don't recognize you,' said Sonali as she turned to her children reminding them, she is Priya *didi.* Give her a hug.' But the twins stood confused. The woman they saw in front of them was too thin, had her hair braided and was wearing a white cotton saree. I kissed them on their forehead, Aashna flinched while Aaryan was indifferent.

My parents escorted their grand children and headed to their chauffeur driven car while Sonali and I walked to the parking lot.

Sonali opened the door to her Skoda Rapid and thundered out of the terminal building.

'My new car sans chauffeur,' giggled Sonali. 'Mum and dad gifted me this car for my birthday.'

'Lovely,' I commented. Sonali rambled about Vinodji as she drove through the crowded lanes, dodging pedestrians, humans on bicycles and bikes. Despite Vinodji pleading to work things out, Sonali was not too keen to go back to the man she had once adored. There had been a shift within her. A shift that takes place when a certain kind of realization sets in. Sonali had realized after ten years of marriage, that Vinodji was not the right partner. Being with Vinodji reminded her of the humiliation and disrespect she faced at her mother-in-law's funeral. She brooded over the times when Karishma remote controlled her mother, the times when Karishma visited her home, took charge of the kitchen while Vinodji stayed indifferent to everyone and everything.

Sonali wanted to forget the unfairness, the misery that she associated with Vinodji now. Something within her had snapped and she walked out of her marriage. Whatever be the reason of their disagreement Sonali had no right to lie to her children that Vinodji was traveling. If they ever found out the truth they would feel betrayed. I listened, analyzed but made no comment. I had to hear the other side of the story as with time I had learned that there are always two sides to a story and the third side is the truth which no one would ever know.

'Your friend Ritika is waiting for you at home,' Sonali announced as we stepped into the elevator of our building. I stared at her. 'Mum thought you would be happy to see your good friend.'

I am neither happy nor upset, just amazed that how mum could take it for granted that I would want to see a friend. Along with my family, Ritika too had been incapable of understanding my feelings. I had stopped responding to Ritika's messages when she had praised Ravi when I had called to talk about my feelings. Ritika suggested that I forget my past, as she believed that I was still in love with Ajai. I had disconnected the line on the pretext that I could not hear her. Ritika had not made a wrong statement but she was supposed to be on my side. I had been a dutiful wife, Ritika had no right to judge me. But she did. And friends who judge are not friends.

We rang the bell to the house.

Supriya stood gaping at me as she opened the door. Embracing me tightly, Supriya wailed. It took her a few minutes to come to terms with the fact, that I was no longer her healthy *didi* .

Mum and dad had reached before us and were chatting with Ritika. Ritika rushed out of the living room and embraced me, 'I am so happy to see you.'

I smiled back as Ritika prattled fervently as to how much she missed me.

Kissing me on my forehead dad excused himself to relax. Dad had not said much but his eyes were red since I saw him.

'Why don't you girls chill in the room while I arrange for some snacks for you all,' suggested mum.

'I would have loved to but I have to take the twins for swimming lessons,' said Sonali as she rushed out holding Aaryan's hand while Aashna followed her mother.

'What the hell were you doing in an ashram?' asked Ritika as we sat on the new metal chairs on the terrace.

I wiped the sweat off my face with the end of my saree. 'Why didn't you tell me?' Ritika demanded.

'I did,' I responded staring into space, 'none of you cared.'

'We did Priya. We were only trying to save your marriage. I never thought that it was so bad,' Ritika defended herself.

'You didn't believe me?' I asked.

'Priya don't take me wrong but we know for a fact that you are short tempered and honestly, I thought that you were still hanging on to Ajai. I am sorry, if I hurt you.'

'Sorry..' I smirked. 'You all are sorry after leaving me alone to fend for myself.'

'I tried contacting you but you were behaving strange. What could I do? And when I asked Radhika aunty she said you were doing fine.' Ritika pulled out a cigarette from a packet. She then offered me one. I refused. Living in the ashram for two months had me give up on smoking, drinking and eating non-vegetarian. Ravi and my differences started with our eating habits and had moved on to spiritual differences.

'The truth is no one cared.'

Ritika rolled her eyes as she lit her cigarette, 'I detest this self pity mode of yours Priya.'

Supriya brought us a plate of *pakodas* and tea. She placed it on the circular table, stared at me, then covering her gaping mouth with her palms, scrambled back to the room.

'You wanna talk about it?' exhaling the smoke through her nose Ritika inquired. 'I know if I pester you, you will avoid me again.'

'I have detached myself from relations. And don't feel the need to share my emotions or ponder on my past,' I responded.

'What the hell Priya! Stop this saintly drama. If you really had detached yourself you wouldn't be loathing in self pity. Come back to the real world and take charge of your life.' Ritika took a puff and sighed.

'How can you call this drama?'

'What else is this? Look at you. You look so weird in that attire. Wearing white and disconnecting with the world is not spirituality. It does not take you closer to God, it takes you away from reality. God has not created humans so that they live in isolation. You are meant to spread love, care for each other, do your duties.' said Ritika.

'You will not understand my reasons. I know how I have suffered,' I let out a whimper.

Flinging her arms in the air, 'You are not the only one who has had to suffer, we all do in some way or the other. We don't give up on life.' Ritika stubbed her cigarette on the parapet, sipped the hot tea and placed it back on the table, 'Call me when you are back to normal Priya.' She then barged out of the terrace as I sat silently. The birds chirped as the clouds gathered in the sky. I sipped on my tea.

******

'You should follow the path, I follow,' said Ravi when I returned from a late evening satsang.
'I feel I relate more to this organization,' I responded.
'But you are my wife, you should follow the path I ask you to follow,' he demanded.
An argument on the right path for me, had led to a massive fight.

'Deepak would not do that,' Ravi said infuriated.
'Are you saying it's me?'
'I don't know, who is speaking the truth,' he had responded.
The truth was Ravi was looking out for an escape from his mistake. His ex girlfriend Taarini was waiting for him.

I woke up to sweaty palms and pounding heart. My throat was parched as I downed a bottle of water. I tip toed to the kitchen to fill up my empty bottle with the torch light on my mobile. Sniveling sounds from the living room caught my attention and I peeped in. A silhouette sat curled on the sofa. I switched on the lights. Startled by my presence, Sonali wiped off her tears with her sleeves. 'What are you doing up so late at night?' she put up a brave face. 'What are you doing here early morning?' I questioned.

'I was not getting sleep and did not want to disturb the children,' Sonali's voice trailing as she gasped for breath.

'You still love Vinodji,' I stated.

'No, I don't care for him anymore, nor does he. He has not bothered to even check on me,' Sonali wailed.

'I am so happy to see you Priya,' Vinodji hugged me tight as we met at a coffee shop unable to recognize me at first.

I had called Vinodji early morning requesting him to meet me for breakfast. Watching my sister cry made me realize that she still loved him but her ego was standing in her way.

'How are you managing?' I asked Vinodji.

'Surviving without my family,' he responded.

'My sister loves you, Vinodji.'

Vinodji as always spoke briefly about his issues, 'Sonali knows how much I love her. Her problem is not me. It is her friends, they have convinced her that her parents can provide a better future for our children.'

'What kind of friends are these?' I asked. I felt a surge of anger arise within me. Sonali had always been surrounded by fair weather friends yet she trusted them more than her own husband.

Bidding adieu to Vinodji I went home with a promise to help him come out of his misery.

Dad and mum had just returned from their morning walk and were freshening up for breakfast. Aashna and Aaryan were getting ready for school and Sonali was preparing their breakfast. Everyone looked happy on the surface. The breakfast table was filled with a variety of dishes, dal pakwan and aloo puri.

'That's a lot of food for breakfast,' I said as I sat at the table.

'These are your favorite,' said mum as she poured the hot chana dal and drizzled it with green chutney. The crispy pakwan melted in my mouth, the moment I bit on it. How I had missed home food! Mum filled up my plate with two puris and the potato bhaji.

'Mum, I cannot eat so much,' I complained.

'Eat beta, I have got this made specially for you.'

Dad smiled, 'Your mother is very happy to have you back. We all are.'

'We are now a complete family,' said Sonali.

'No, we are not.' responded Aaryan dropping his fork back on the plate. 'Dad is family too.'

******

Sonali lay in bed reading to her children. Aaryan had been cranky since morning and continued being so even after he had returned from school. Sonali had managed to calm him and feed him dinner. But she knew that he would not give up.

I tip toed and lay beside Aaryan as Sonali finished reading Peter Pan. Aaryan had dozed off, his face pale and exhausted after all the crying. Aashna asked her mother to read her the story of Cinderella. Sonali complied with her daughter's wish, flipping through the huge story book.

Cinderella, the story of a young girl who loses her mother and is ill treated by her step mother and sisters after her father remarries. The mother and sisters trouble Cinderella but she faces those hardships with a smile and a hope that her life will soon be better. Her desire to attend the ball is fulfilled by her fairy god mother. Cinderella arrives at the ball in a carriage wearing a beautiful gown. The prince is enticed by her beauty and asks her for a dance. Cinderella rushes out of the palace at the stroke of midnight and drops her glass slippers. The slippers that helped the prince find the woman he had fallen in love.

Aashna was now fast asleep.

Sonali and I walked out of the room.

'Cindrella has been my favorite fairy tale since I was a child,' I said as I poured hot green tea into the cups. Sonali picked up her cup and stood by the wall gazing at the night sky.

'A love story that makes you want to believe in happily ever after,' said Sonali.

'A rags to riches story,' I sighed as I sipped the tea, 'but today I realized that it also has a spiritual side to it.'

Sonali raised her brow.

'A family that lives happily till the mother dies. Father

marries a woman with the hope that she will fill their life with happiness. Reminding us that things don't always go according to our plans.'

Sonali responded with a 'hmm,' as she gazed at the twinkling stars.

'Cinderella's life is filled with hardships but think about it, she still goes through it with a smile. She does not give up hope as she goes about doing menial housework.'

'How is it spiritual?'

'Cinderella is disciplined and humble. Despite the evilness of her step sisters and mother, Cinderella has faith. Faith that good will come. Reminding us that we need to face the adversities in our life with a smile. Her faith in the Universe was blessed with abundance in her life. The wicked step mother is our ego that obstructs our path to success. We are all like Cinderella, there will be obstructions but we need to stick to our path, our duty. Abundance and love will follow.'

******

I opened my room door to mother who was frantically searching for Sonali. Sonali was nowhere to be found. Dad had checked with the watchman regarding the last time he saw Sonali, but he had no idea. He had been sleeping on duty. Mum suggested, we check the security camera recording but dad asked her to relax. I too tried dialing Sonali's number but it was switched off.

Last night, Sonali had been staring into space for a long time when I asked her what if in the fairy tale the prince had rejected Cinderella. She then abruptly walked out of the room.

I had meditated till late night and then dozed off till was woken up by mother who was banging at my door at eight in the morning.

I dressed the children to take them to the club for swimming, as their mother had promised them that she would in the morning.

'Are you coming with us?' Aashna stared at me.

'Yes, mum has asked me to take you both,' I responded.

Aashna's innocent wide eyes stared at me, 'You cannot come like this with us.'

I walked towards the long mirror in Sonali's room. A scrawny looking woman with eye bags, dressed in a faded white saree and wavy hair stared back. Ritika was right, I looked miserable.

I emerged from my room half an hour later. 'Let's go swimming *masi*,' said Aaryan. Aashna gave me a peck and said, 'You look nice.'

I discreetly looked around in the club hoping to see Sonali. The twins jumped into the shallow side of the pool with their floats. I dialed Sonali for the tenth time hoping she had switched on her mobile. Mum's name flashed and I answered on the first ring. 'Sonali has left her mobile at home. I found it in her drawer.

The battery had died. I have kept it to charge,' mum rambled. My heart was sinking. I felt guilty. Did I say something to upset her. Images of Sonali on a railway track, in the deep sea floating were popping in my mind.

Aashna stepped out rushing towards me followed by Aaryan. 'We want to go home to mama and papa,' Aashna wept. I hugged them tight. In the pool were parents playing with their toddlers.

The day had gone by entertaining the twins, while mum and dad frantically called friends and family. No one knew where Sonali was. I had been trying hard to curb myself from visualizing any negative thoughts but they were like bubbles that kept surfacing in my mind.

Outside the day had turned to dusk. Aaryan and Aashna refused to eat dinner and were not interested in the iPad or television, all they wanted was for their mother to return. How I wished that I had asked Sonali to sleep with me in my room last night, like when we were children. We would stay up all night gossiping and imitating common friends and our teachers, playing ludo and dressing up like mum. We would steal her *dupattas* and make up and pretend to be her. The time when we shared our thoughts, our feelings. But as we grew older we drifted apart. We cared and loved each other but we were no more best friends.

At nine o'clock the door bell rang and we all leaped

towards the door. Sonali and Vinodji stood hand in hand. My first reaction was of anger but when I saw the children's happy faces, my anger dissipated. 'We are going home,' said Vinodji to the twins.

24

"'Let your good deeds be like rain. Drop a little everywhere."
- Abdelilah a Albanee

Paintings of indigent children adorned the cream walls of Ritika's office. Situated on the eighteenth floor, the windows of her organization had a swanky panoramic view of the city. A palpable divide of the sky scrapers in the skyline, alongside the dilapidated buildings and shabby hut settlements; a view that well defined Mumbai.

The innocence of the children visible in their twinkling eyes, their skin scorched from the strong sunlight. With a backdrop cement, tartar and bricks the children looked intently at the person observing them. The signature below had Ritika's name. Envious and yet proud of my friend who spend every moment of her life creatively and passionately.

After a few minutes of our the meeting, Ritika's assistant barged into the office. There had been a mishap at the construction site and the builders were not ready to pay for the child that had been hit by a speeding car just outside the site.

'Is he bleeding too much?' asked Ritika.

'They said, Motu had a narrow escape he might have fractured his leg,' replied Dorothy.

Ritika immediately tapped on her mobile, waited for the other person to answer and then instructed him to be by the family's side and provide them with whatever cash they needed.

'We can go to the hospital if you want,' I suggested.

'No, he is with his parents and is being taken care of. I will go to see him tomorrow.' Ritika responded as she checked her mobile.

Ritika informed me that she had twenty mobile schools at construction sites.

'You have schools at construction sites? Why?' I asked.

'The construction industry in our country is the largest employer of migrant laborers. Laborers who travel from one area of work to another along with their families and most of them come from West Bengal. Around one million, men and women work in this sector. Do you know how much these laborers earn in a day?'

I nodded as Ritika continued, 'Only fifty to hundred rupees a day, while a woman worker earns around sixty rupees a day. The working conditions at these sites are inhumane, living on construction sites in tents that are built out of rubber and metal sheets. They have no access to clean drinking water and toilets.'

'That's terrible. I had no idea.'

'Priya, these children wander around aimlessly, while the parents work during the day. This is the reason I started this NGO. I work in collaboration with corporates, the government and the builders. We are fighting for their right to a safe environment and access to education.'

'It's sad that those who build these buildings, malls, hospitals and homes for people have to live in misery.'

'Isn't it difficult to handle all this?' I asked.

Ritika was not only socially active, she ran an NGO, painted and also traveled extensively.

'Nothing is difficult if you put your mind to it Priya. I have sponsors, friends and even many strangers who donate on our website. I have to face a lot of obstacles but I take them in my stride and move on. Complaining about problems does not give you any solutions.'

'Don't you stress? I mean wouldn't you rather be in a meditation retreat or live in the Himalayas,' I asked.

'By working with these children, I am contributing to the society. When you live in the Himalayas or escape into retreats you are only helping yourself. You can live in isolation for some time but not all your life. And there is no greater joy than the joy of giving,' responded Ritika.

'How can I contribute to the society, when I haven't received anything myself. I have been destined to suffer.'

'We take more, than what we can give back to the

society,' said Ritika, 'there are women who have experienced far worse than you have.'

'What can be worse than your husband doubting your character?' I asked.

'Forget your past Priya. Help me with my social work,' said Ritika, 'we have partied enough and lived our lives, let's go out there and help those who need us.'

25

"Not everyone is meant to stay in your life forever.
Sometimes they are only there long enough to teach you
the lessons that you needed to learn." - Anonymous

The obituary read,

'*R*am *Kewalramani' passed away peacefully on 17-03-2018. Deeply mourned by daughter- Karishma Makhija, son-in-law- Madhav Raj Makhija, brother -Sham Kewalramani, sister-in-law- Sarojini Kewalramani, and niece-Amit and Angeli. The condolence ceremony will be held on 19-03-2018 from 5:00-5:30pm Lok kutir, Khar(w). No condolences thereafter.*

I read the obituary then reread it in the hope that my eyes were deceiving me. But what I was reading was true. I was one of the spectators to a broken home.

Sudha had once told me that *'vinaasha kaale vipreet buddhi,'* when one's destruction time is near, one's thinking is clouded. Karishma's thinking had been clouded by her greed and ego and she had no clue.

Dad and mum were practicing pranayama on the terrace when I handed dad the paper and his reading glasses. Dad's face turned pale as he forwarded the paper and his reading glasses to mum.

Vinodji sat in the living room with moistened eyes, his hands trembling as he held on to the newspaper.

'What's the matter?' asked Sonali who had returned home after dropping the twins to school, 'what are you all doing here this early and why are you all dressed in white?'

Vinodji, let out a sob.

Sonali trembled as she embraced Vinodji.

'Why is no one telling me?'

I handed Sonali the newspaper.

Sonali slumped on the sofa.

Mum began beating her chest and wailing. 'Mum can you calm down please,' I whispered.

As soon as I had calmed mum, Sonali began wailing, 'How could she do this to her own brother? What is she out to prove?'

'She will burn in hell,' mother proclaimed. My family was not grieving the loss of Mr. Kewalramani. They were grieving the loss of humanity.

Through a large gold frame, Mr.Ram Kewalramani smiled blissfully. The hall was filling in with family and friends. We walked towards his picture and paid our reverence.

Karishma was seated on the designated seats for the family along with other family members. Her eyes outlined with kohl and lips tainted a shade of light pink. However hard Karishma tried to camouflage, her evilness could not be hidden beneath the layers of foundation that she caked herself with. She flinched in her seat as Sonali walked up to the family designated area, greeted them courteously and sat amongst them.

The prayer meet ended with the priest sprinkling the holy water first on Vinodji and then on the rest. Vinodji and Sonali stood up to thank the mourners who had come to convey their condolences. Karishma barged out of the hall.

******

Ordering myself a glass of orange juice and a sandwich, I relaxed by the pool at the club after an intense yoga session. Exercising had triggered the feel good hormone within. I was in a happier place than I had ever been. I squinted as my eyes gazed at the blue sky, feeling gratitude for everything in my life.

'Hello Priya Wadhwani,' said a familiar voice. I looked to my right. Samar, wearing a body tight t-shirt and track pants was standing beside me.

It had been a while since we had spoken to each other. I had been so consumed with my life that his existence had stopped mattering to me.

'What are you doing in Mumbai? How is your father?' I asked.

'I am back in Mumbai as I lost my father to cancer a

few months ago,' said Samar as he pulled up a chair and sat beside me.

I felt guilty not knowing about Samar's father's death. But how would I know when Samar had fizzled from my life.

Samar had reconciled with his wife Amrita. 'We are working on our marriage,' he said. He spoke about their visit to the marriage counselor, his undying love for his wife.

'How is your husband?' asked Samar as I stood up to leave.

'I am divorced,' I responded.

Friends meet, spend good times with each other and often grow apart. Something within me had snapped. I no longer felt a connection with Samar. With a prayer in my heart, wishing him happiness and love, I bid him goodbye.

I walked through the rocky pathway to the sounds of drilling and hammering. This was the fifth construction site I had visited since I joined Ritika in her social work. I looked up at the incomplete sky scraper, the sight had me queasy, men working on the site, without helmets or any safety net to protect them. Leaving my slippers outside the make shift school on the site, I entered the damp room that had been divided into three areas.

A crèche for babies and a pre-primary section for children between the ages of three and five. Around ten children above the age of five sat in a circle with a slate and chalk as they copied the Hindi alphabets that the teacher had written on the board. The children greeted me with a warm smile and a 'good morning' as we introduced ourselves to each other. In total, there were ten children, out of which six were girls and four were boys. Their eyes sparkled with joy as I informed them that I would be teaching them English. A lanky boy wearing a checkered short sleeves shirt and khaki shorts raised his hand.

'Yes Majeed,' I said.

'I know little English, but like learning lot. Happy you teach.'

'I am happy to know that you all are excited to learn.'

I handed them worksheets with the alphabet A.

26

"The real guru is the pure intellect within;and the purified,deeply aspiring mind is the disciple."
- Swami Chinmayananda Saraswati

'Initiation by a Master, makes life's journey easier,' grandfather had said when I was a teenager. As a teenager nothing matters more than physical and material needs.

Despite the long hours of meditation and a positive approach to life, I felt a deep void in my soul. On some days I felt, I had progressed and on others I felt I was going nowhere with my meditation. I was battling with my thoughts, my desires and my emotions. Master had returned from Haridwar and I had approached him for spiritual guidance as I had been unable to concentrate in my meditation.

'Why is it so difficult to meditate Master?' I questioned.

'Our mind is a mischief maker. It wants to distract you because it detests discipline. It will lure you into thinking about the future or reminiscing the past so that you don't focus on the present moment. Thoughts that will scratch the surface of the deep buried emotions. Emotions of hurt, resentment, anger, lust, ... just so that you are not in the present.'

'I practice meditating daily but at times I feel I am not going anywhere with it, I want to attain self-realization.'

'Meditating on a guru mantra will help you focus better,' said the Master. 'With constant *naam japa* you will attain mental purity. The mantra will act as a ladder to God-realization.'

'Will initiation by a Master, help me attain my goal?' I asked.

'Initiation by a *Guru* is the fastest road to salvation. But only if the *Guru* is himself true to God.'

The bells of the *durbar* were a signal to follow my thought. There was no other perfect Master than the man who stood in front of me.

I followed the Master to the morning *aarti*.

'Please initiate me,' I pleaded as he lit the *diya*.

The Master sat in silence in his room, his dark tuft of hair tied in a bun.

It took two weeks for Master to respond to my request for initiation. I had visualized this moment every day and night. The Master had called for me early morning. I knelt in front of him seeking *naam daan*.

Touching my forehead with his two fingers he shut his eyes. Blessing me and preparing my soul, with a surge of divine energy that trickled through every cell in my body. Whispering the *guru mantra* in my ear the Master announced me as his disciple.

His *chela* handed him a *rudraksha* rosary which he touched on his forehead, recited a mantra as he held it next to his eyes and then handed it to me. I had watched my grandfather thumb his rosary for hours and I was excited to own one. I was following my grandfather's wishes of serving the *durbar* he had been attached to for life.

******

'A fashion show will help you raise funds and attract attention from the media,' dad suggested at the dinner table.

I called Ritika, to share the ides. 'That's a good suggestion, work out the numbers,' said Ritika over the phone. Ritika was attending a meditation retreat in Himachal.

'Ritika, but my parents have no idea how it is done nor do they know anything about NGO's or fashion industry for that matter,' I rattled.

'We underestimate our parents. Don't forget they survived without Google and they did pretty well for themselves. Why don't you google 'fashion shows' and get some ideas. We need funds Priya. Find a way. I have to hang up Priya, it's meditation time,' Ritika disconnected the line.

******

Ameesh Chopra's workshop was chaotic. Models

trying out fittings, dressmakers attending to the last minute changes. Ameesh had created a beautiful collection from Rajashtani textiles. The workmanship of each garment was supervised by Ameesh. *Dabka, Danka, Kota dori, laheriya, Baagru* were terms that I heard for the first time.

Six months of research, traveling and sleepless nights had brought us closer to our dream project. Ameesh had agreed instantly when mum approached him to help us in our cause. Traveling with us to villages in Rajasthan and guiding us as we purchased textiles and appointed karigars. Namita, my petite assistant had nose dived into the project with great enthusiasm from the day of her appointment.

I walked into Ameesh's cabin. He was sitting with his head on the desk.

'What's the matter Ameesh?' I asked.

'Anaita and I broke up this morning,' announced Ameesh.

My heart was pounding and my mind whirling Anaita Irani, the top model was to be our show stopper. Did that mean she would not participate in the fashion show. The media was expecting to see her in Jaipur the day after tomorrow. I geared my thoughts to the present moment. I was being selfish. I was worried about the show but here in front of me sat a man who had just been heart broken.

'She just messaged me that it was over between us. Can you believe it Priya? You think it is normal?'

It was normal for today's tech generation, I wanted to say but refrained. All I could do at this moment was listen to him but Ameesh took his sweet time to fill me in. All I wanted to know was if Anaita would be participating. If she wasn't then our show was doomed.

Hunger and nervousness within had my stomach growling. Ameesh dropped the bomb.

'Anaita is not going to be our show stopper. You will have to find someone else,' he said scrambling to his washroom.

How did Ameesh expect me to find a show stopper two days prior to the show? Why couldn't he keep his ego aside and behave like a professional.

I called mum, Sonali and Ritika. All had the same answer, 'convince Ameesh.'

The sanctum was serene and quiet, unlike the noise I had experienced ten minutes back at Ameesh's workshop. The sanctum had become my solace whenever I was agitated and unable to think. I pulled out the rosary from my handbag and thumbed it, as I mentally chanted the mantra that had helped me overcome many a hurdles through the project. When one prays with devotion and belief the answers to one's questions appear. I had an answer to the prevailing problem. I hesitated at first but the answer was loud and clear and I had to follow it with faith.

I scrolled my contact list to find his number.

27

"The weak can never forgive,
Forgiveness is the attribute of the strong"
- Mahatma Gandhi

'When you become an angel, with your vibrations you will make others an angel too,' Master had said when I once complained about the builders who refused to help with funds. The habit of complaining about others, was what stunted one's growth and only when one changed did others change.

I had been following Gaurav, on social media as he hobnobbed with politicians, film personalities and anyone rich and famous. While I meditated on a solution the only images that played on my mind were of Gaurav's instagram posts. Whether it was my inner voice or my mind that had been deceiving me I was not sure, but anyways I dialed his number. Gaurav took a long time to answer and within those few seconds I relived the pain, the humiliation that Gaurav had inflicted on me. I had tried hard to delete Gaurav from my memory, the pain had thinned with time but not healed itself. Healing occurs only when one is able to forgive. Just when I was about to disconnect the line he answered.

On receiving my call the first words that Gaurav uttered were, 'I am sorry for what I did.' His kind words had burnt the residues of the pain.

'Sorry', when uttered with compassion and honesty touches the heart of the victim, healing it forever.

We spoke for a long time, reminiscing the good times I had long forgotten. The good moments outweighed the painful ones, yet I had only one memory of my ex.

He disconnected the line with a promise to help the NGO.

In an hour's time I had received a call from Natasha Singh's secretary. Natasha Singh had risen to fame after her first film. Young, ambitious and dynamic. The incident reminded me of what Sudha had said to me, 'When something does not go the way you want it, remember God has better plans for you.'

A *guru's* blessing helps extinguish the flames of ego that corrupt the mind.

'You spoke to Gaurav?' Ritika asked for the fifth time.

'Yes Ritika,'

'I can't believe it! Natasha Singh will be our show stopper,' screamed Ritika over the phone.

'He also has transfered five lakhs to our NGO.'

Silence.

'And we thought he was evil,' said Ritika.

'We all evolve,' I stated.

Two days prior to the show, we arrived with a bang at Jaipur airport. Our flight had landed with a velocity that had our hearts in our mouth and in those few seconds we had experienced death closely. The strong winds made it difficult for the pilot to land, his first attempt failed and he immediately flew the aircraft back into the clouds. Circling around for a while and then with determination and speed he landed on the tarmac of Jaipur International airport.

Ameesh and Ritika rode with my parents in one cab while I hopped into another cab with the twins, Sonali and Vinodji. While dad, mum and I had visited Jaipur umpteen times in the last six months, the children were visiting the royal city for the first time. Popular for its rich culture and heritage Rajasthan had blown me away with its opulent palaces and forts.

'*Masi* we want to sit on the camel,' said Aaryan 'my teacher said that I would be able to ride on a camel in Jaipur.'

'Of course Aaryan we will,' I pecked him.

'I want to visit the forts,' said Aashna. 'We learned about the Amer fort in our class.'

'Once *masi's* show is over we will take you for camel rides and show you palaces and forts,' said Sonali.

'You are also a part of it, Sonali. You are the senior make up artist for our show,' I responded.

'I don't know why you have dragged me into this. I am a novice artist.'

'Although you are novice, you are brilliant at your work. Isn't she Vinodji,' I asked

'My wife is the best in whatever she does,' said Vinodji.

Sonali blushed.

'Mum is the best,' the twins rattled.

We arrived at the four star hotel that had opened its doors to our organization and sponsored the event. Thanks to mum's social standing we had a lot of sponsors backing us. The hotel arrangements were organized by mum's present good friend Bina. 'You saw how networking helps,' my mother had beamed with pride. Dad and mum had been my pillars throughout the planning stage. Never ever, had I seen them so close to each other as they were now.

Ritika supervised the carpenters as they prepared the ramp while Ameesh rested. The anchor for our show was shortlisted and was waiting at the lobby. Slender built, dark long hair, Jamini introduced herself. Jamini had anchored many events, shows and weddings. Ten minutes of the meeting and I was impressed with Jamini's inputs on the itinerary that I had mailed her.

We had planned for the *karigars* to attend the event and felicitate them. We were discussing the idea of placing them around will help promote their work when we were interrupted by someone shouting out my name.

I looked around.

A portly man wearing mustard trousers and checkered orange and blue shirt was bolting towards me.

We embraced each other for a few seconds, the smell of mustard oil from his hair, bringing back memories of Ajai's wedding.

'I came here to buy tickets for the fashion event and then I find out, that Priya Wadhwani is in charge here.'

'My NGO is organizing it. We are a team,' I corrected Rakesh.

'I read that your show stopper is Natasha Singh.'

'She is,' I blushed.

'Please I want to see her. I want to meet her, touch her,' Rakesh's expression had me hysteric.

'Come for the show. I will arrange for you to meet her, but no touching,' I laughed.

Rakesh then went on to ramble about how much he missed me but was unable to reach me.

'My number has changed,' I responded.

'Mine hasn't,' Rakesh complained, 'you never kept in touch,' his lips pursed.

Jamini coughed as a reminder that she was waiting.

'Type in your number on my phone,' I handed my mobile to Rakesh. He typed in his number and name as Rakesh, Ajai cousin.

'I need three passes,' Rakesh was back after two minutes.

I grinned and made a note to arrange for three passes as Jamini and I discussed the event.

'How long are you here till?' Rakesh yelled from across. I lifted my three fingers.

'We must meet for lunch or dinner shouted Rakesh.'

'Who is this cartoon?' asked Jamini.

'A dear friend,' I smiled.

******

The day unfolded smoothly and everything was running as per plans till Namita, my assistant for the event, dropped a bombshell on me.

 Namita quivered as she updated me.

'Natasha Singh is here, she has been allocated the Maharani suite, the models too are here, so are the assistant make up artists and hairdressers.

'Good,' I responded. 'Make sure they rest and report four hours prior to the show. Except for Natasha who will be getting her make up and hair done in her suite.'

'Ma'am there is a problem,' Namita's body oscillating from left to right had me dizzy.

'What's the matter?'

'I had booked Nat...asha Singh's pers...onal make up artist and hairdresser on another f.....light.'

'And.'

'That flight has been delayed by six hours.'

'Delayed?' why?'

'Tec...hnical problem,' Namita slumped on the sofa and covered her face with her palms as she sobbed.

'It's not your fault why are you crying,' I consoled Namita sitting beside her on the large floral printed sofa.

'Natasha Singh is very particular about her makeup. She might not walk the ramp if her make up artist does not arrive.'

'Relax Namita, we will find a solution.'

Namita had been in Jaipur since a week sorting out things and making sure that everything was in place on our arrival. There had been no hiccups beside the Anaita fiasco and now this. But my mind had already made a plan. All I had to do was convince Natasha Singh.

Dressed in track pants and a plain white t-shirt Natasha welcomed me to her suite.

'So nice to meet you in person,' said Natasha as I introduced myself. My eyes fixated at this Greek Goddess. I had seen her pictures and watched her movie but none of them had been able to do justice to this diva. Her true essence lay in her glimmering eyes. Eyes that radiated love and compassion.

Natasha was aware of the fact that her make up artist and hairdresser would not be able to make it in time for the event yet, she was composed.

'We sincerely apologize, but some things are not in our hands,' I said.

I pulled out my mobile from my trouser and showcased Sonali's work.

'I know your make up artist is experienced but I can assure you Sonali will do a fabulous job. Please give her a chance,' I pleaded.

The lawn was fast filling up with guests, the volunteers were gearing them towards the workstations.

While back stage was chaotic. Ameesh yelling at his assistant, models giggling and smoking.

'I don't want my collection to smell of dope and be careful of those lipstick stains,' screamed Ameesh,the models couldn't care less.

Flood lights were dimmed as the Audio Visuals of the organization's body of work was screened. Jamini dressed in a Rajasthani ghagra and choli went on to call Ritika, the founder on stage. Ritika spoke of the project and thanked me, my family, Ameesh, Natasha, our sponsors and the volunteers.

The fashion show commenced with the DJ playing retro music to which the models strutted on the ramp. Natasha Singh, the show stopper dazzled the crowds with her gold smoky eyes matching her zardosi gown.

She held Ameesh's hand and then mine and walked back towards the crowd. We all bowed, my heart fluttering with joy. Ameesh spoke a few words and passed the microphone to me.

I felt a sudden surge of divinity within and on the front seat sat my parents, their face lit up with joy. Then there were no bodies just lights flickering in the lawns, on every chair was a speck of light, some bright and some dull.

28

*"The mystery of human existence lies not in just staying
alive, but in finding something to live for."*
- Fyodor Dostoyevsky

I stood with the microphone in my hands, staring at
the silhouettes. Silhouettes that were transforming
into specks of light. There was no me, there was no
them. We were all one.

Ritika embraced me praising me for my choice of
words. 'You were good, I don't know why you had
refused to speak on stage.'

People were walking upto me and Ritika and pledging
their support. I touched my parents feet who had been
waiting patiently for me. 'You and Ritika deserve a big
hug,' said mum as she embraced us both. Dad kissed
us both on our forehead. 'It's so good to see the youth
of today strive for a better society.'

Sonali and Vinodji were in a conversation with Rakesh
and a lanky man and a woman wearing a headscarf.
Rakesh was wearing a mauve *churidar* and a black
kurta. When would he get his clothes right, I thought to
myself. Sonali saw me waving at her and she bolted
towards me.

Sonali embraced me tightly thanking me, while I thanked her for helping me and doing a great job. Natasha Singh had offered Sonali to work with her for important occasions. 'No work is too small, you must accept it Sonali, not for the money but for your passion,' I said, my eyes were fixated on the deep hazel eyes who was sauntering along with a frail woman wearing a headscarf. My heart was beating faster and faster.

'Priya we are so proud of you,' said Vinodji as he bolted towards me. 'Ajai was just telling us that he knows you.'

I smiled at Ajai as we shook hands. 'How are you *beta*?' asked Kamini. Kamini's hands trembled as she caressed my cheeks. 'I am fine aunty, how are you?' I asked. 'Surviving with Guru Baba's grace,' she said.

Rakesh embraced me ,'I am waiting for you to introduce me to my dream girl.'

Sonali intervened, 'Come I will take you to her.'

I sat on the bed physically exhausted while my active mind relived the events of the day.

Mum had requested Kamini to join us for a Rajasthani meal in the hotel. Although Ajai had refused, Kamini insisted Ajai to join in. Ajai had complied to his mother's wish. Rakesh sat beside me at dinner filling me in, about his life. He had not yet found his missing sister but lived in hope. While Rakesh chattered my mind was focused on chewing my food the sweet and sour yoghurt curry, the sour tomatoes in the soft potato bhaji, the spicy mixed vegetables, the soft ghee rotis.

'Priya,I am sorry for judging you. I have realized it's not the color of your skin or size that matter but the purity of one's soul. You are a pure soul,' Kamini hugged me tight as she slid into the car. Ajai kissed my hand and sat beside his mother. Rakesh hugged me tight, thanking me for fulfilling his wish. 'Don't delete my number, ever again.'

The evening had been memorable. The moment that had struck me the most had been the one on stage. That moment was perfect. Was it my Master's grace? Was it Master who spoke the words that I never did? Would I relive this moment ever again?

My mobile rang.

'Are you awake Priya?' asked Ritika.

'All okay?' I asked.

'Come to the lobby now,' said Ritika disconnecting the phone.

Why was Ritika asking me to come down at eleven in the night. I slipped into my track pants and hastened towards the lobby.

Ritika had been sitting beside Ajai at dinner. Was it something to do with Ajai. Did Kamini collapse? Did something go wrong at the event? Was there some issue? Did the media criticize our show?

Too many negative thoughts, I corrected myself.

Ritika stood in the lobby, wearing the red bandhini saree that Ameesh had gifted both of us. We had twinned this evening.

'You changed?' asked Ritika.

'You don't expect me to be sleeping in a saree, do you,' I responded.

'Were you meditating?'

'I was self contemplating and reflecting,' I yawned.

'I was with Ajai and we had a nice long chat.'

'Ok,' I responded, 'good for you.'

'He wanted to talk to you before he left for London.'

'Talk? About what?' I asked.

'World economics, I guess,' Ritika smirked. 'Ajai is a great guy.'

'Thanks for telling me Ritika.'

'He is waiting for you?'

'Where?'

'By the lawns. I had asked him to drop his mother and come back to meet you.'

'Why Ritika?'

'He still loves you Priya.'

I walked towards the lawns. Ajai sat on the white marble steps gazing at the twinkling stars.

'Hi Ajai,' I sat beside him on the steps.

'I am sorry to wake you up,' said Ajai.

'I was awake.'

I waited for Ajai to fill in the silence. 'I am sorry Priya, sorry for not fighting for our love.'

I listened.

'Sonakshi could not accept the fact that I had cheated on her on the eve of our wedding.'

'You told her what transpired between us?'

'Yes..'

'Why?' I asked. The emotions that I had erased from my blueprint had resurrected themselves and were consuming me with guilt and shame.

'I had to speak the truth.'

'Silence would have been a better choice.'

'I could not live with a lie all my life,' said Ajai.

'You should have thought of it before you circled around the sacred fire.'

'I was bound by my duty. My mother emotionally blackmailed me at that time.'

'Your mother did wrong by forcing you.'

'She believes she has been punished for her wrong deed.'

'God does not punish, our actions do.'

A waft of breeze engulfed me with Ajai's scent. On the screen of my mind I was reliving every beautiful moment spent with Ajai. Our first meeting, our friendship, the love I felt for him, the feelings, emotions, excitement. I felt it all.

'You faced a lot of hardships in your marriage too,' Ajai stated.

'I experienced what I had to,' I responded.

'It must have been painful,' said Ajai sliding his fingers into mine. My body responded with a tingling sensation and I curled my fingers around his.

'It's all in the past. I don't think about it anymore,' feelings of guilt that were resurfacing had me uncoil my hand instantly.

Ajai lifted my chin, his penetrating warm hazel eyes staring at me. I drew in a deep breath. Ajai pressed his warm, soft lips on mine and kissed them tenderly. A wave of lust along with feelings of past guilt were flushing through my entire body. Caressing my neck Ajai whispered into my ear, 'Marry me Priya.'

I froze..........

EPILOGUE

'*I will wait for you till eternity,*' *Ajai had sighed that evening as he walked away. I had experienced one broken relationship after another to feel fulfilled but none had lasted. The one relationship I believed in did not stand up for our love. Was I ready to accept the man who had rejected me over duty? I could not find the answer.*

'*Why would you want to go to the mountains?*' *mum had questioned when I had woken them up early morning wheeling my trolley bag.*

'*Why Ladakh of all the places, it had a flash flood a few years back. It's not safe,*' *dad had pleaded.*

'*I don't fear death,*' *I responded.*

'*You were getting back to normal, what happened to you again.*' *Mum pressed her hand on my forehead checking if I had fever. *'*Why do you get these sudden impulses to run away?*'

'*I am not running away mum. I am informing you where I am going.*'

Dad suggested I talk to Master. I had spoken to the Master, 'listen to your inner voice,' he had responded.

'How long are you going for?' asked dad.

'I don't know, a week maybe or a month. Till I find my answers.'

'Please tell...'. Before mum could say anything further, dad intervened, 'If that's what your heart says, but please take care of yourself.'

'I never understand you Priya. When all is going so well for you, you have a good job, you are doing good social work and suddenly you decide to go to the mountains,' whined mum as she hugged me tightly.

'Let her go, she is an adult. We cannot control her life,' said dad pecking me on my forehead.

I had trekked with strangers in the snow-clad mountains for a week. The biting cold and long hours of walking would leave me physically exhausted by my mind rambled in the silence of the icy mountains. Ajai had only come back because his wife left him... would he have returned if Sonakshi had decided to stay on.....was Kamini suffering because she hurt my feelings?

I lived in a monastery for a month seeking answers to my questions on life, on relationships.

'The mind is like a bag of mustard seeds, if you spill the seeds on the floor, it is hard to pick up again. But if you use a vacuum cleaner you can easily collect them. Concentration is the key to clearing the restless thoughts,' the monk said as I left the monastery to spend time in the valley and meet the Ladakhis.

The tittering in the room and the warm hugs from

the children whom I visited twice a year, elevated my soul. Two years had past by since I met these Ladakhi children. Some were only three years old when they had lost their parents in the flash floods. The school had been funding two hundred orphaned children. I had opted to sponsor twenty children who had now become my family.

'You promised to bring your friend this time,' said Stenzin scrunching her face as she stood behind the wooden round table surrounded by twenty children that our NGO sponsored. Tashy, our eldest adopted child and a national champion in ice hockey pressed the candles gently on the cake.

'Shall we light the candles?' I asked the children loudly ignoring Stenzin's grievance. I could not lie and neither break her surprise. Stenzin picked the knife from the table, her eyes fixated at my hotel room door. This was their favorite chocolate cake from Delhi which I brought, every time I visited but today was special as it was Stenzin's birthday.

I leisurely lit each candle, scanning each one of my adopted children. As soon as I lit the sixth candle the door to my hotel room unbolted. Swinging it open, 'Happy birthday to you, happy birthday to you,happy birthday dear Stenzin, happy birthday to you.' Ajai sang as he sprinted towards Stenzin, his adopted daughter.

'The man who has given up all desires, who desires nothing, not even this life, nor freedom, nor God, nor work, nor anything. When he has become perfectly satisfied, he has no more cravings. He has seen the glory of the self and has found that the world and the Gods and the heaven are within his own self. There the gods become no gods, death becomes no death, life becomes no life. Everything has changed.'
Swami Vivekananda.